FATHER MALACHY'S MIRACLE

CLUNY CLASSICS

RICCARDO BACCHELLI
The Mill on the Po: God Save You (BOOK ONE)
The Mill on the Po: Misery (BOOK TWO)
The Mill on the Po: Nothing New Under the Sun (BOOK THREE)

ROBERT HUGH BENSON
Come Rack, Come Rope
Dawn of All
The Light Invisible
None Other Gods

GEORGES BERNANOS
A Bad Dream
A Crime
Joy
Under the Sun of Satan

ORESTES BROWNSON
Like a Roaring Lion

MALACHY G. CARROLL
The Stranger

G. K. CHESTERTON
Wanderings over the World

MYLES CONNOLLY
The Bump on Brannigan's Head
Dan England and the Noonday Devil
Mr. Blue
The Reason for Ann & Other Stories
Three Who Ventured

ALICE CURTAYNE
House of Cards

GERTRUD VON LE FORT
The Pope from the Ghetto
The Veil of Veronica

JOSÉ MARÍA GIRONELLA
The Cypresses Believe in God (TWO VOLUMES)
One Million Dead (TWO VOLUMES)

RUMER GODDEN
A Breath of Air
Five for Sorrow, Ten for Joy
In This House of Brede

CAROLINE GORDON
The Life and Passion of Aleck Maury
The Malefactors

NATHANIEL HAWTHORNE
The Shattered Fountain: Selected Tales

ELISABETH LANGGÄSSER
The Quest

BRUCE MARSHALL
Father Malachy's Miracle

FRANÇOIS MAURIAC
The Dark Angels
The Desert of Love
Genetrix
A Kiss for the Leper
The Lamb
The River of Fire
The Unknown Sea
Vipers' Tangle
What Was Lost

DOROTHY L. SAYERS
Whose Body?

IGNAZIO SILONE
Fontamara
Bread and Wine
The Seed Beneath the Snow

SIGRID UNDSET
The Burning Bush & The Wild Orchid
Four Stories
Images in a Mirror
Madame Dorthea

LEO L. WARD
Men in the Field: Eighteen Short Stories

FATHER MALACHY'S MIRACLE

A Heavenly Story with an Earthly Meaning

Bruce Marshall

CLUNY
Providence, Rhode Island

Cluny Media edition, 2021

For information regarding this title
or any other Cluny Media publication,
please write to info@clunymedia.com, or to
Cluny Media, P.O. Box 1664, Providence, RI 02901

VISIT US ONLINE AT WWW.CLUNYMEDIA.COM

ISBN: 978-1685950095

* * *

Cover design by Clarke & Clarke
Cover image: N. C. Wyeth, *Blubber Island*,
1938, oil on gessoed panel
Courtesy of Wikimedia Commons

TO
MY WIFE

this the crystallization
of a few thoughts
which came to me on a green omnibus

I should like it to be clearly understood that none of the characters appearing in this novel are portraits of persons living or dead. It is, of course, true that some of their follies, philosophies, and foibles have been compiled from my observation of actual people and that my personal knowledge of the subject and the district about which I have written has made the dead bones of my imagining rise up and live; but it is the peculiar privilege of the novelist to piece together the patterns of life which he finds thrown at his feet, and unless he were to take advantage of the material thus afforded him no good books would ever, I am afraid, get written. (For life is good literature escaping just as surely as good literature is life held fast.) I admit, then, that I have grafted onto my puppets the human ambitions, decencies, and weaknesses without which they would not have walked or talked; but I would stress, for the information of the scandal-mongering and the uncharitable, the fact that I have brought them to print by combining different characteristics which I have observed in different human beings and not by using a camera.

BRUCE MARSHALL

"Sure," said Father Neary, "and miracles are intoirely out of fashion these days. If one were to take place in His Lordship the Bishop's bedroom the Right Riverend ould gint would be after hushing the indaicency up."

FATHER MALACHY'S MIRACLE

CHAPTER I

1.

ONE foggy morning in November a little old clergyman in a shabby black coat got into a third-class compartment of a train waiting in Queen Street Station, Glasgow, disposed his ancient brown bag on the rack, sat down, shut his tired old eyes the better to rid himself of the world, and began to meditate upon the folly of all human ambition and the wisdom of Almighty God and of the love of Our Lord Jesus Christ and of the way that the Holy Ghost went about the world, now blowing like a wind, now taking the form of a flower and glowing in gorgeous reds and yellows.

Outside, on the grey ribbon of platform which ran dismally along the side of the train, newsboys were pushing on wheels pyramids of the contemporary literature, gay magazines within whose covers Ethel M. Dells and E. M. Hulls split their infinitives and modern deans argued as to whether twin beds in matrimony were of the *esse* or merely of the *bene esse* of the sacrament. Outside, boys were selling sticky sweets and cigarettes and porters were pushing luggage and flabby, colourless people were jostling one another with impatience as though their departure for Falkirk or Edinburgh were important and as though the dreadful immortality of their souls shone out, for all to see, through the pigginess of their earthly faces. Outside, Queen Street Station, Glasgow, looked just as depressing as the Gare du Nord, Paris, and suggested, just as adequately, milk cans, lavatories, and eternal damnation. Outside, Queen Street Station continued to be Queen Street Station.

A fat man climbed into the same compartment as the little clergyman, a fat man with a face that was so red and pouchy that it looked like a bladder painted to hit other people over the head with at an Italian carnival. He sat down, or rather threw himself down, in the corner opposite the priest and began to read a pink paper in which the doings of horses and erotic young women were chronicled at length. He was followed by a middle-aged woman who had a peaky, shiny nose with a funny little dent in the middle and whose hat was one of those amorphous black affairs which would have been, at any moment, out of fashion in any country.

The priest was distracted from his meditation. It was impossible, he told himself, with a wry little mental smile, to think competently of the Father and the Son and of the Holy Ghost proceeding from Both, with such a bulging red face in front of him and such a peaky, peering woman placing her parcels here, there, and everywhere. How hard it was, here below, and with the material and the temporal crowding out the spiritual and the eternal, to love one's neighbour, how hard and yet how necessary. For the soul behind that bulging red face had been redeemed by Christ just as surely as had his own, and Our Blessed Lord, while He hung on the cross, had seen the funny little dent in the middle of the peaky, peering woman's nose just as clearly as He had seen the broad, bland visage of Pope Pius the Eleventh and, so merciful was He, loved it just as much. And yet it was difficult to imagine bulge or dent in heaven unless, among the many mansions, there were one which should be one-tenth Beatific Vision and nine-tenths Douglas, Isle of Man. Of course, if it came to the point, it was difficult to imagine the majority of contemporary humanity in any paradise which did not syncopate Saint Gregory and whose eternal sands were without striped bathing tents and casinos.

He closed his eyes again. If he must love his neighbour he would love him without looking at him. He closed his eyes, and not only did he close them, but he kept on repeating the reflex action in his brain so that, with the bulging red face and the peaky, peering woman, away went the compartment, the train, the station, the world; and, as Scotland went swinging after Scandinavia and Spain came scampering after and Australia flew to join the stars, he was alone with God.

A great nothingness was before him, a great nothingness that was Something, a great nothingness that was All; and in the warm freedom from the tangible he knew his Saviour and was absorbed by Him.

2.

OUTSIDE on the platform, where men knew God only as a metaphysical conjecture and heaven as a geographical uncertainty, porters continued to trundle barrows and young girls to rush about in coloured sweaters and flying skirts just as though Father Malachy Murdoch, priest of the Order of Saint Benedict, had not, by closing his eyes and letting his mind spiral, annihilated them, their barrows, their sweaters, their thoughts and their aspirations. They continued, that is to say, to have an objective existence, to be independently of anyone else's knowing or not knowing that they were, to mirror for their moment on earth the Will that had called them up out of nothingness, to trundle their barrows and rush about in coloured sweaters just as though Descartes had never said "*Cogito; ergo sum*," and David Hume been skeptical of the reality of his own *ego*. And they thought, those hurrying, scurrying folks, of whether the tip would be sixpence or merely threepence, of the way men kissed in dark corners at dances, of whether Mexican eagles would rise another point or two, of whether Bobby So-and-So would go round North Berwick in under seventy and of how, if pigs couldn't fly, Colonel Lindbergh could; and they thought not at all, those hurrying, scurrying folks, of Socrates and of why he had drunk the hemlock, of Jesus and of why He had been nailed to the cross.

But Father Malachy, alone with God in a third-class smoking compartment of the London & North Eastern Railway, knew their thoughts, although he did not know them, yet knew them not as Isaiah said that Jehovah knew the thoughts of the children of Israel, knew them rather kindly, for he was a monk and a priest forever and had drunk Christ's Blood and raised up, morning after morning and with trembling, uncertain hands, Christ's poor, battered Body and because he loved, so truly Christian was he, his neighbour as himself. He knew, and knew with gentle pity, all their follies: all their silly lustings in secret places, all their silly jazz and broadcastings and speed trials which made them think the Trinity such poor fun, all their silly interpretations of all the silly scientists which made them think the Trinity such poor geology, all their prideful belchings of opinion, all their imaginings that comfort was civilization and sin a mediaeval name for taking away for a weekend an actress to whom you were not married, all their petty conceits, all their superstitious rationalisms.

He had been sent, had Father Malachy Murdoch, by the abbot of the Benedictine monastery at Fort William, to instruct the priests and people of the Church of Saint Margaret of Scotland, Edinburgh, in the use of the Gregorian chant. And here it may be as well to point out, for the instruction of those who imagine that ritual is absurd when ordered for the worship of God and reasonable when applied to the comings-in and goings-out of lord mayors and transatlantic film actresses, that Saint Benedict and his followers have always been of the opinion that the service of the temple is of greater importance than the service of the market and that it is, in view of eternity, more sensible and indeed more dignified to consecrate all stateliness and pageantry to the Almighty Father than to petty princes and princesses who strut their hour and are forgotten almost before the click-clack of their heels has died away on the boards of the somewhat irregular platform which Shakespeare called a stage. But, be the Benedictines right or be they wrong, Father Malachy Murdoch, being of their number, was persuaded that they were right and, as he wished the good Catholics of Edinburgh to love the worship of God at least as much as they loved the theatre and dancing, he had been glad when the abbot had called him aside one morning after the Conventual Mass and said to him: "Father, I know that you look like a monkey and that at first sight it would seem that you had precious little dignity in your bones; but I know also that you are the best *ceremoniarius* that Scotland has produced since that horrible piece of open sin called the Reformation and so I want you to pack up your traps and chasubles and go to Edinburgh where a priest who calls himself the Very Reverend Shamus Canon Geoghegan is trying to instruct his consecrated hobbledehoys of curates in the difference between entering the sanctuary and the grandstand at a football match." He had been glad and he had answered with a very good will: "Yes, Father Abbot, I'll go."

But it was not of the Very Reverend Shamus Canon Geoghegan and his liturgical ambitions, nor yet of the people in the compartment with him, nor of the odd million in the city about him that he thought as the train jerked itself out of the station and began to pound, snort-a-snort, along the forty iron miles which separated Glasgow from Edinburgh. For, as has already been pointed out, Father Malachy Murdoch was meditating upon God and His existence and His absolute attributes. And so, as the train went clanging through time and space, he pondered the mystery of miracle and of how absurd it was that men should deny to the Creator the power of doing what He would with His creation. For it was surely evident that He Who had ordered the tides should also, if the caprice should take Him or if there were souls to be saved that way, be able to disorder them and that He Who had commanded the sun to move should be able to command it to stand still. Nay, more, was not the miracle of sequence more marvellous than the miracle of the interruption of the same sequence? Was it not more marvellous that, when one woke in the morning, one's coat was still hanging over the back of the same chair than it would have been if, during the night, God had caused it to be transferred to a scarecrow in Russia? More marvellous and more kind. And it needed, as the theologians said, just as much of a miracle on the part of God to conserve the world as to create it or to destroy it. The fact that mountains and tram lines and telegraph poles remained where they were was just as miraculous as Christ walking on the Sea of Galilee or the feeding of the five thousand. For as the earth spun round before God He poured His Will over it so that it might continue to be the earth and cattle to get up where they had lain down. *Omnia,* as Saint Thomas Aquinas had pointed out, *exibant in mysterium.*

Such was the pondering of Father Malachy Murdoch, of the Order of Saint Benedict, as the train trundled him along to Edinburgh; and the gentleman with the bulging red face scratched his ear and rustled his paper and decided that, if Hot Dog didn't run, Pink Nightie would be a dead cert, for the two-thirty.

CHAPTER II

1.

THE Very Reverend Shamus Canon Geoghegan was a dry Irish-Scottish cleric of about fifty-two years of age who had recently been appointed by the lord bishop of Midlothian, in whose diocese the parish was situated, as rector of the Church of Saint Margaret of Scotland. His predecessor had been a fat and tubby and thoroughly Scottish priest, a Hamish Canon Buchanty, who had been loved by and had loved the Lord's poor and whose mortal remains had been followed to their last resting-place by seven bishops and seven thousand women with shawls over their heads. But Shamus was, in the idiom of these parts, a very different cup o' tea from Hamish: Shamus, like Manning, had priest written large upon his brow and walked about the aisles of his church with a hoity-toity quasi-liturgical sway as though he were, forsooth, an ecclesiastical mannequin parading chasubles in the *salons* of some spiritual worth; Hamish, like the holy, undignified old barrel that he was, had rolled onto the sanctuary in carpet slippers and said Mass nonetheless effectively for all that: Shamus was tall and thin and had black eyebrows of the type that are said to beetle, and never laughed if he could possibly look severe; Hamish was short and stout, an advertisement for porridge and the Grace of God, and had never looked severe if he could possibly laugh: Shamus was all for the observance of the *minutiae* of liturgy; Hamish had hoped, not unreasonably, that God wouldn't notice a few mistakes: Shamus considered that modern dancing and short skirts were purple sins; Hamish hadn't seen much harm in a hop now and then and in the lassies, bless their hearts, showing a bit of ankle or even, on the greater festivals, a bit of knee as well. Yet, such is the mission and such the might of that Church which consecrates a coolie just as surely as she does a king's son, both were equally untiring in their ministry and both believed (although now one of them walked no more by faith) with equal sincerity all that the Catholic Church has proposed for acceptance by her children whether they be Spaniards or Frenchmen or Chinamen or subalterns in the Grenadier Guards.

"Ha," said Shamus, when he received Father Malachy in the dingy brown parlour of the presbytery, "so you've come, have you?"

"Yes," said Father Malachy, "I've come."

"Pleasant journey?"

"Quite, thanks."

"Sit down, won't you?"

Father Malachy sat down on the edge of a very uncomfortable-looking chair and rested his hands, palms downwards, on the knees of his shiny black trousers. Canon Geoghegan, who was wearing one of those long sacklike coats affected by the Catholic clergy in England, flicked upwards that portion of it which ordinarily concealed his rump and placed himself gingerly on a chair opposite and folded his hands in front of his non-existent paunch. For the moment both priests seemed all black boots and superseded theology.

There was one of those silences which are nevertheless articulate enough to tell people who don't know one another well that they don't know one another well.

"The lord abbot of Fort William..." The canon rolled out the words as though they were celestial thunder from the Psalms. "The lord abbot of Fort William told you exactly why I required the services of one of his monks for a few weeks?"

"Yes," said Father Malachy. "I understand that you are trying to introduce plain chant into your church."

"Trying, yes." The canon smiled a cold little smile, which died almost before it was born. "Believe me, these young curates which I have are not the best material to work on. Maynooth may teach theology, but it doesn't teach table manners, Almighty God's table manners, I mean. Any Irish priest is incapable of behaving like a gentleman in the sanctuary until he is thirty-five. And as the Irish bishops only loan us their youngest and roughest and then haul them back to their native dioceses as soon as they have learned to behave with moderate decency..." He left his sentence to finish itself in the mind of his hearer, then added: "And, of course, old Buchanty let them do just what they liked."

"I have always heard Canon Buchanty spoken of with respect and generally with affection," said Father Malachy.

"Quite." Canon Geoghegan wore the expression of a dentist being forced to listen to a dentist praising a dentist. "Of course, he was loved. Gave money to news-vendors down on their luck and all that sort of thing. He was Scots, too. Not just Portobello Scots, but the real thing. He came from Inverness and used to preach as though he were wearing a glengarry instead of a biretta. And that made him go down with the Protestants. But he had no idea of liturgy or rubrics."

Father Malachy nearly expressed his opinion that news-vendors down on their luck would be more grateful for sixpences than for liturgy or rubrics; but he remembered in time his rule of being charitable even to the uncharitable and said nothing.

"So you see, the tradition's bad. Mixed choir and scrambled ceremonies, Roman chasubles and dirty albs. Of course, I'm going to change all that: I'm going to introduce a surpliced choir, teach my curates dignity, and lay in five full sets of Gothic vestments. It will take some doing, I know, but I'm going to do it even if the bishop disapproves."

"But surely," said Father Malachy, "the bishop will be only too glad if you succeed in beautifying the services of your church."

The canon made a grimace which said, without saying: "Will he hell?"

"My dear Father, I am afraid that you don't know the bishop. I am only speaking the truth when I say that he doesn't give a snuff about ritual and that, as far as music is concerned, he doesn't know the difference between 'God Save the King' and 'Pop Goes the Weasel.' And he wears his mitre as though it were a tam-o'-shanter, all higgledy-anyhow. He's the sort of priest that would like to say Mass in a tartan chasuble on the anniversary of the birth of Burns. No, my dear Father, we can't expect much backing from the bishop."

Father Malachy thought how sad it was that even priests bound to teach the same truths in the same heedless Scotland could not love and understand one another and of how very ultimately alone and dependent upon God was every human soul. Men talked of nations and corporate consciousnesses of various sorts; they didn't exist; there were only individual souls, imaged by the Father and superscribed by the Son, trying to pretend that they were essential parts of something greater than themselves, and all, apart from the Trinity and the Hierarchy of Heaven, ridiculously, appallingly alone.

"I understood that he was a very famous bishop," he said gently. "A convert to the Church, isn't he?"

The canon nodded.

"Oh, he's famous all right and a convert, a little too famous, perhaps, and a great deal too much of a convert. What the Church wants is bishops born to the Faith who will settle down to their job of distributing the Holy Ghost and not waste half their time letting off controversial fireworks with Presbyterians. These converts are no good." The canon looked blandly out from behind his glasses as, in one short sentence, he banished Newman, Manning, Robert Hugh

Benson, Gilbert Keith Chesterton, Ronald Knox, and his own Father in God. "Always shouting about the light that they saw on the road to Damascus and forgetting to turn about and set their faces for the New Jerusalem. In any case, no man who's ever taken seriously the Church *of* Scotland ought to be allowed to become a bishop of the Church *in* Scotland; it's as bad as trying to make a dancing girl pious."

Father Malachy, who was a gentle soul and loved to see the good in people rather than the evil and who kept ever before his eyes Our Lord's command to love the sinner whatever the sin, was very unhappy and quite at a loss how to reply to the canon's indictment of converts and dancing girls. If he had felt justified in following his own inclinations he would have said nothing; but he decided, after duly considering the matter in the light of his conscience, that to be silent would be to shirk his duty and to sin from motives of human respect.

"I am sorry to disagree with you, Canon," he said. "In my opinion, the converts have been a signal grace granted to the Church by Almighty God. When I was a boy I once went to the Oratory in Birmingham and saw Cardinal Newman say Mass and I'll never forget it as long as I live. You could see his faith and love and wisdom in every movement he made. No, my dear Canon, I am all for converts. And I seem to have heard quite a lot about dancing girls who went to Holy Communion every morning of their lives."

He sat back and blinked, for he was a nervous man and was somewhat dismayed at the thought of the explosion which he imagined would follow. But he need neither have sat back nor blinked, for the canon, with a kindly smile, came forward and, leading him gently towards the window, said:

"Perhaps you are right, Father, and perhaps I spoke rather bitterly. Newman, I know, was a great man, a very great man. And how sad it is when one reflects upon how quickly greatness, true greatness even, is forgotten. I am afraid that the majority of my people would say, if questioned as to the occupation of Newman, that he was a billiard player." He gave a sharp little laugh which was entirely humourless and which was as different from a real laugh as a put-on cough is from a bronchial cough. "But I think that you must allow me to say that, in my opinion, you are mistaken about dancing girls, about dancing girls in Edinburgh, at any rate." He pulled aside the brown curtain which shut out from the room the outer world where men bought and sold and ate pork chops. "Do you see that building opposite?"

Father Malachy looked and saw a church with a placard outside it, on which was printed, in red and blue:

BRING
YOUR GIRL
TO
EVENSONG

"It's a church, isn't it?" he asked half turning to the canon, half re-reading the poster.

"Not *that* opposite," said the canon. "That, I admit, is a church of the Scottish Episcopalian heresy and commonly known as an 'English' church by Presbyterians who are unable to pronounce 'Episcopalian.' The rector is one of those unfortunate schismatics who can't get a congregation together without resorting to the methods which have made Bovril a household beverage. No, it's the *other* opposite I mean. A bit to the right. Just beyond where that lorry's standing. It's really not opposite at all, but I have grown so used to referring to it in my sermons as 'that flaunting Babylon opposite' that I have come quite to accept the idea that it is really opposite and not, as it is in actual fact, at a distinct angle of forty-five degrees."

Father Malachy looked and beheld, wedged in between a tea merchant's premises and a lawyer's office, a building which seemed, at first sight, harmless enough and which consisted, like its neighbours on either side, of three stories, all equally depressing and matter-of-fact. Indeed, but for a dome of coloured glass above the entrance, it might have been a reflection of the presbytery mirrored on the surface of a rather misty lake.

"I am afraid that I don't understand," he said slowly.

The canon explained:

"That building with the coloured glass above the door has caused more scandal in my parish than all the seven deadly sins put together. It is what is known in bad French as a *palais-de-danse* and furnishes accommodation, music, and girls for young medical students who wish to perform the inartistic and, to my mind, repulsive motions which contemporary thoughtlessness describes as dancing. And, not content with supporting short skirts and bare arms and shaded corners, styled locally *squeezitoria,* it flouts revelation by calling itself the Garden of Eden." The canon snorted. "Mind you, I know what I'm talking about when I say that the place is a hotbed of iniquity. My bedroom happens to be the room just above this and when the place vomits forth its faithful at an early hour in the morning I don't half see some carryings-on." His eyes glinted hardly and humourlessly behind the thick lenses of his metal-rimmed glasses. "The Babylonians at least had the decency to believe the finger when it wrote on the wall. But these people would refuse to pay any attention if Almighty God Himself walked into the dive and painted MENE, MENE TEKEL UPHARSIN in pentecostal scarlet upon the ballroom floor."

Before Father Malachy had time to say anything or, indeed, to wonder what he was going to say (for he believed, like all men of good will, that dancing had its purposes just as spiritual exercises had theirs and that both could be abused) he felt his arm seized from behind and heard the voice of Canon Geoghegan squeaking excitedly:

"Look. Do you see that little man and the girl coming out of the Garden of Eden? I'll bet you a new breviary to a medal of St. Anthony of Padua that you don't know who *that* is."

"I have always made it a rule never to bet unless I am certain of winning," said Father Malachy. "But let me have a good look just for the fun of the thing and then I'll see if I can guess."

The canon stood back a little and, without turning round, Father Malachy was conscious of the holy leer on his sleek, shinily shaved face. But he looked, just for fun, as he had said to the canon, at the man and the girl who had come out of the Garden of Eden and were now, arm-in-arm, crossing the tram lines and laughing together as though they were glad to be alive. The man, who appeared to be about forty-five years of age, was wearing a blue serge suit, a grey bowler hat cocked at a rakish angle, and white spats which, so very white they were, reminded Father Malachy of nothing so much as a pair of newly baptized souls; the girl, a fluffy young inconsequence of nineteen or twenty, had golden hair and was dressed in the silken flimsiness of the hour.

"I've no idea who they are," he said after he had thoroughly seen them. "But they certainly do seem very happy."

"Happy!" The canon was again at his elbow, flattening his nose against the window pane and breathing mists of hot air all over the glass. "Happy! I should think they are. But do you know who they are? Do you know who the man is?"

"I've already told you that I don't," said Father Malachy. "I am a stranger to Edinburgh, you must remember."

"Well, the man is the bishop's brother." The canon shot out the information with gleeful sorrow. "The Bishop's Bad Brother or the Bee Bee Bee, as he is known in every presbytery and public house in the diocese."

"Dear me," said Father Malachy. "Is that so? And is he really bad?"

The canon waved his arms in a gesture that was almost Gallic.

"You ask me that after what you have just seen? My dear Father, the man's behaviour is a positive menace to society. To begin with, he is an unbeliever of that school which states that God is to be found on green golf courses and underneath blue skies just as much as in cathedrals which they are pleased to describe as having 'massive golden altars.' And he is famed for the amount of alcohol he can put away at any single sitting and for his promiscuous association with gay young women who earn their living by dancing. And everyone knows that he's the bishop's brother."

Father Malachy kept nodding his head.

"I see. And that girl he's with now is a gay young woman?"

"Certainly. She's one of the official instructresses attached to the Garden of Eden. I expect that she's just been giving him a few lessons in the foxtrot or the tango or whatever they call it. My sacristan tells me that in the mornings from eleven to one they give 'tuition in terpsichorean deportment' at the rate of five shillings an hour."

"She looks a nice, bright young thing," said Father Malachy. "Perhaps she isn't as bad as you make out she is."

The canon looked at Father Malachy with a questioning gleam in his eye.

"My dear Father, I haven't been a priest for thirty years without learning that pretty women who earn their living by dancing are—well, pretty women who earn their living by dancing. And now, if you've quite finished looking at the young lady in question, I'll take you upstairs and introduce you to Fathers Neary and O'Flaherty."

2.

Meanwhile, as spiritually remote from their observers and commentators as they would have been physically if they had been in Siberia, the Bishop's Bad Brother and his companion continued slowly and happily on their way to the grill room of the North British Station Hotel.

"Bubbles," said the Bishop's Bad Brother, "your eyes are as sweet as bluebells."

"Sugar Daddy," said the little lady at his side, "you're not half a bad sort, really."

The Bishop's Bad Brother swung his shoulders with pleasure and wriggled his whole body as a tomcat does when he is caressed.

"Bubbles, I'll stand you a dry martini for that. Two dry martinis. And three if you'll say that you love me more than Mandy Condison."

Bubbles, who was not, as the French say, a dancing instructress for prunes, pressed herself, cuddlingly, against him and droned:

"Sugar Daddy, I love you more than all the men in the world. Cut my throat, cross my heart and see all the rest of it, I do."

And the Bishop's Bad Brother, feeling that the cup of his happiness was filled to overflowing and heeding not the prim matrons and lawyers of these parts, sang out above the booming of the electric trams:

"Nachum nachum nu
Nachum nachum norus
Nachum nachum nu
And that's the heilant chorus."

Somewhere in France solemn-faced men were sitting down to discuss the payment of reparations and three hundred yards down the street Father Malachy was telling Father O'Flaherty that the Irish had indeed kept burning the sanctuary lamps of the entire world. But Bubbles and her Sugar Daddy neither knew nor cared about reparations and sanctuary lamps; they were happy and, in their happiness, sufficient unto themselves.

CHAPTER III

1.

ABOUT twenty minutes to eleven on Sunday the faithful of the quarter began to enter the church for the eleven o'clock High Mass. These faithful included Irish labourers and their families, Italian ice-cream merchants and their families, French mistresses from some of the more exclusive girls' schools, a flock of Belgian nuns, a few university lecturers who had been converted to Catholicism by reading history or theology, a handful or so of Real Ladies and Gentlemen who saw no inconsistency in accepting both haggis *and* Papal Infallibility, and a horde of publicans whose piety would have shamed a Carthusian monk. They came, all of them, to comply with the universal precept of the Church and to gain comfort and strength from worshipping with their fellow Catholics in a land the majority of whose inhabitants imagined that the Apostolic and Roman Faith was a superstition specially minted for the delusion of Hibernian domestic servants. All around them the MacWhirters and MacGregors were preaching that humourless brand of Christianity which is supposed, for some reason or other, to produce good surgeons and competent accountants, and the good surgeons and competent accountants, disdaining that which had made them what they were, were off to Barnton, Luffness, or Muirfield to worship the Trinity in unity by going round in under eighty. But the faithful of the quarter held fast to tradition and they had, those of them who thought very deeply about the matter, the satisfaction of knowing that, if they were out of fashion in Edinburgh, they were at one with the high nobs in Madrid and Ventimiglia and with that gang of toughs subsequently known to hagiology as the Apostles.

In the sacristy (that kitchen where the hieratic mysteries are so unmysteriously prepared) there was a froth of men and boys sliding into surplices and cottas and Canon Geoghegan was pushing his baldish pate through an alb and looking very much like an irate farmer going to bed in a Christie comedy, and Fathers Neary and O'Flaherty, who were to be deacon and subdeacon and who were already vested in their green tunicles, were having a *sotto voce* conversation about electric hares, and Father Malachy, who was to preach the sermon, was walking up and down with his hands folded beneath his scapular in the manner approved by his holy father Saint Benedict.

"Father," said Canon Geoghegan as he began to fasten the girdle round his waist.

"Yes, Canon," said Father Malachy, slipping silently to his side.

"About that sermon of yours." The canon spoke in an earnest whisper. "Pitch it in strong. First of all, the dignity of plain chant, Gothic chasubles, and all that, and how all this polyphonic nonsense is in direct opposition to the wishes of His Holiness. And then the Garden of Eden. Details, you know. Sex music, silk stockings, and unbridled passion. Late hours and good young Catholic girls being led astray. And then contrast the tum-ti-tumness of the modern dance with the chaste harmonies of St. Gregory. Pile it on. And if you notice anyone sleeping preach *at* them until they open their eyes."

"But surely, my dear Canon, I can sufficiently justify the seemliness of performing the supreme act of worship in a decent and chaste manner without dragging in the establishment on the other side of the road. And it's not as though I had had much experience of preaching on vice. You see, I live all the year round in a monastery and all the preaching I do is to priests in retreat and an occasional Sunday sermon to the Highland laity who, as you must have heard, are most virtuous and not at all attracted to the things which you have just mentioned. Why not leave the subject over until your annual mission? The Redemptorists do that sort of thing so very much more competently than I could ever hope to do." Father Malachy did not speak these words without reflection for, so quickly does the human mind flash across whole continents of logic, philosophy, and fact, he was able, in the second of time that cradled the interval between Canon Geoghegan's question and his reply, to weigh Christ's love for the sinner against Christ's hatred for sin and to decide that, in this instance at least, all references to a pastime which was not *per se* evil would be out of place and might do more harm than good.

"But, my dear Father," Canon Geoghegan droned in his most wheedling voice, "you must surely see the scandal that such an establishment causes in my parish? Most of our young men and, I regret to say, many of our young women frequent it and are thereby led into occasions of sin. And their temptation is made the more grievous by the fact that, Saturday night after Saturday night, they see the brother of his lordship the bishop in a state of intoxication and indulging in wanton familiarities with indecently dressed dancing instructresses. I take a pride in the souls as well as in the sanctuary of my parish, my dear Father, and, for every sermon I have preached on the ornaments of the altar and the ministers, I have preached two on immoral novels and walking down dark lanes after ten o'clock at night. Please, Father, do not lose this opportunity of helping me to carry out the work which Almighty God has called me to do."

Father Malachy thought again, quickly, deeply. Like an invisible machine his mind loosed its own controls and went chasing down the channels which it had hewn for itself in the dark, uncharted lands of interior consciousness. Dancing halls, he knew, were not always run in accordance with what the hierarchy called in their pastorals truly Christian principles, and shaded lights and southern music and short frocks often fanned to a blaze those passions which the moral theologians said were more responsible for the peopling of hell than all the other sins put together. And yet was it by suppressing dance halls that one would usher in the reign of Christ? Was it not rather by preaching the old story of the Passion and Crucifixion of Christ Our Saviour that one would kill those longings which made it so hard for men and women to remain pure? And, from a which-came-first-the-egg-or-the-chicken point of view, was it not the passions which caused the dance halls rather than the dance halls the passions? If people could only be got truly to love God they would find such pleasure in kneeling before the Blessed Sacrament that they would require neither dance halls nor cinemas nor theatres. If... There was unbelief and there was hatred and there was apathy. But the way to kill them was to preach Christ and His love. Dance halls were but the least of all the stumbling-blocks. No, he understood the canon's feelings all right, but he could not do this thing which was asked of him.

"Please do not think me obstinate or unsympathetic, Canon," he said, "but I really must ask you to excuse me from a task for which I am not fitted by nature."

The canon pulled the cope round his shoulders with more of a rustle than was necessary.

"As you will," he said crisply. "I suppose that I shall have to crack the whip myself at Benediction this evening."

"I think, perhaps, that that would be the best way out of the difficulty," said Father Malachy, and could not, for all that Saint Paul had said about charity, resist adding: "After all, it's your circus, isn't it?"

2.

THEY poured away; the scratch beginnings of the new choir, the acolytes, the sacred ministers poured away out of the sacristy onto the sanctuary where, with many posturings and posings, they began to re-enact the drama of Christ's Blood shed for the redemption of men.

Father Malachy, who, as has already been indicated, was a very holy old man and a very simple old man, was not of that multitude of priests who say their own Mass and never put in two minutes' prayer at any other priest's Mass; yet he did not follow the procession into the church because he wanted to be alone and to gather together his ideas for his sermon. And in any case, as the sacristy door had been left open, he was morally present at the Holy Sacrifice and could hear the mumbled "*et vobis, fratre*" of Canon Geoghegan as, with a twist to right and to left, he confessed to Almighty God, Saints Peter and Paul, Fathers Neary and O'Flaherty and Mrs. McGinty in the back pew that he had sinned exceedingly in thought, word, and deed, through his fault, through his fault, through his own most grievous fault.

So, gathering the ample folds of his Benedictine cloak about him, he began slowly and silently to walk up and down the sacristy and to ask the Holy Ghost to put words into his mouth. For that was his method and he had never, in forty years of priesthood, known it to fail. He asked for inspiration and he handed on the inspiration which he received. He did not spend hours in the preparation and the committing to memory of long jeremiads or exhortations. And when he preached he spoke rather than orated, so that everyone in the church thought that they were alone with him. Hearing Father Malachy preach was rather like going to confession, so much a spiritual *causerie à deux* did it seem; and it left on the soul a great peace, as mountains do when the moon is on them and lakes when they catch and refract the starlight.

And as he walked up and down, up and down, he knew that the world was a very wicked place and that in Buenos Aires young girls were seduced in their teens and that in Paris most men had mistresses and that here in Edinburgh things weren't very much better. He knew, too, that in New York men cared more about money than salvation and that in Hollywood cinema actresses were not as simple as they seemed. He knew these things in virtue of his being a man among men and he knew them again as he paced the sacristy. But he knew also that there was much unseen virtue in the world and that it didn't get talked about as vice did because it had less gossip value. He knew, in his quality of priest, that there were many unknown saints of God on the earth whose fame would not be noised among men until time should have passed into eternity. He knew, too, that there were many queer people, following queer avocations, who loved God just as much as Saint Teresa or Saint Francis or the Little Flower had done: tight-rope walkers, tram drivers, surgeons, sailors, cardinals even. And, as he knew these things, the good and the bad, and knew them over again, he gave great thanks to God Who had ordered all things wisely.

If only men would believe in God and love Him and keep His commandments... If only they would do these things, then, Father Malachy was old-fashioned enough to think, there would be no more wars and no more rising up of nation against nation, no more envy, no more vain ambition. If only the countries of the world would learn to think in terms of grace instead of in terms of coal. If only... Ah, there was the trouble. In the nineteenth century someone had started the rumour that God wasn't God and that Christ wasn't Christ and that sin wasn't sin and ever since then there had been no way of doing with people at all, at all. Dancing halls and local Babylons and girls with naughty little twinkles in their eyes there had always been. Indeed, they had been to practical Christianity very much what bunkers were to golf courses, the hazards that made the game worth playing. But nowadays when people sinned they said they were doing right and that young men must be young men and that everyone was entitled to be as immoral as everyone else. And it was no use handing the sacramental niblick to people who didn't believe in unsacramental bunkers. The proprietors of brothels, he reflected dryly, ought to pay a royalty to the professors of exegetics. Unbelief. That was the root of all evil.

Ah, but these dear people weren't unbelievers, these dear O'Raffertys and D'Agostinos and O'Shaughnessys; they believed all right, were Catholics in a city and in an epoch which regarded their holy religion as sanctified flummery and an insult to the intelligence and all the rest of it. Poor dear O'Raffertys and D'Agostinos and O'Shaughnessys, how Our Blessed Lord must love them.

And so it was that, when Father Neary had brogued out the notices and announced that on Tuesday evening there would be a mission for Eyetalians which every Eyetalian in the parish must attend, he went up into the pulpit and, spreading out his arms so that his cloak fell as a cloud about him, preached on the Love of God which, he said, was as strong as steel beneath blows and as gentle as oars being dipped in still waters.

CHAPTER IV

1.

To many Father Malachy's preoccupation with the supernatural will no doubt seem foolish and, in these days when Mr. H. G. Wells and Mr. Arnold Bennett have finally exploded the prophets, unscientific; but it must be urged in his defense that, having lived for nearly fifty years in a monastery, he knew nothing of modern theo-geology, contraception, book-keeping by double entry, broadcasting, taking the creed with a pinch of salt, chorus girls, chorus deans, talkies, aëronautics and all the other without-which-nots which are the pride of our glorious contemporary civilization. For Father Malachy, poor little man, was content to believe that Christ had meant what He said and remained unmoved by the assertions of prominent company promoters that He had meant the exact opposite. And he really imagined, in these wonderful post-war years when every butcher boy is entitled to be his own pope, that Christianity was literally and wholly true and not just a musical way of spending Sunday mornings and evenings. So that the many, no matter how well educated they are or how often they have spoken English to French waiters at Deauville or how much they may disbelieve in the New Testament miracles which they can't name, must, I am afraid, be indulgent and realize that this chronicle is, in effect, the story of a very mediaevally minded man living in modern times and unable to understand, through the blindness which those who are afflicted with it call Faith, that stock exchanges have taken the place of cathedrals and that no rational man can be expected to stomach doctrines acceptable only to prize noodles like Saint Athanasius and Hilaire Belloc.

And what is true of Father Malachy is also, in a lesser degree, true of the clergy of the Church of Saint Margaret of Scotland. For Canon Geoghegan, although he, as he himself would have phrased it, knew a thing or two (some of the more worldly of his cure used to say that they got quite amusing tips from his sermons) believed that birth control was wrong and that divorce was equally wrong and that far-seeing men like Dean Inge and Sir Harry Lauder were talking through their hats when they told their Sunday publics that one religion was as good as another. Indeed he was most fierce in his condemnation of what the majority of people regarded as sanctified by public approval and, Sunday after Sunday, he would anathematize with equal zest Presbyterianism, flesh-coloured stockings, pajama parties, and any modern novel in which the characters behaved as though they were really alive. And Fathers Neary and O'Flaherty, two raw bonny priestlets if ever there were two, would consign straight to hell fire anyone who missed Mass on Sundays or caused scandal to the young by reading the pernicious and scabrous works of Joseph Hocking. Still, be they right or be they wrong, the fact remains that the priests and people of the Church of Saint Margaret of Scotland lived their own peculiar life in a district populated for the most part by loose women and chartered accountants and that, in spite of enlightenment, progress, and motor transport, they confessed and were confessed, distributed and received what they believed to be the Body of their Lord just as though it were the fourteenth century and England still merrie and Scotland not yet stern and wild.

For a few weeks after the events narrated in the previous chapter things went on very much as usual. That is to say that the loose women continued to be loose and the chartered accountants to imagine that their profession was learned and Canon Geoghegan to hate the Garden of Eden and Anglican bishops in council and Fathers Neary and O'Flaherty to administer the Sacraments with the stolid efficiency of chemists selling pills. In other words, Edinburgh continued to be Edinburgh just as London continued to be London and Paris to be Paris. For places and the people in them do not change very much and, although all over the world there are movements to convert the impure to purity and the unbelieving to belief and the stupid to intelligence, the great variety show goes on as ever and men living next door to one another are as far apart as though five oceans lay between them. And, this being as true of the parcel of space occupied by the parish of Saint Margaret of Scotland as of that occupied by the parish of Nuestra Senora del Mar in Barcelona, it is exceedingly improbable that this story would ever have been written had not Father Malachy, one Friday morning, the ninth of December, chanced to rescue the top hat of the Reverend Humphrey Hamilton, rector of the Episcopal church on the other side of the street.

It had been arranged, by agreement between the lord abbot of Fort William and Canon Geoghegan, that Father Malachy should remain with the latter until the end of the month of February, by which time it was hoped that the choir would have learned to chant in the Gregorian tone and Fathers Neary and O'Flaherty to observe the rubrics in a manner pleasing to Almighty God. And so, on this particular Friday, the ninth of December, Father Malachy, having said Mass at nine and breakfasted on a kipper and a boiled egg at ten, was walking past the heretical church of Saint Ninian's and looking, in his battered black felt hat and shabby coat, as unremarkable and ineffectual a clergyman as you could find in any other town. But, inside, his mind was all rosy and golden, for he was meditating as usual upon the Love of Our Lord, and it remained rosy and golden until, summoned from meditation by the church notice board which obtruded itself upon his gaze, he read:

COME TO EVENSONG.
IT'S CHEAPER
THAN
THE PICTURES.
GOD DOESN'T MIND IF YOU HOLD HER HAND.

At which Father Malachy's mind became as black as the coat which was flapping about his legs because, being a monk, he was ignorant enough to find something distasteful in advertising divine service as though it were marmalade or a Chrysler Six. And, as he stood there and disapproved, a well-dressed clergyman came out of the church and the same wind as was responsible for the well-known epigram of Robert Louis Stevenson caught at his hat, raised it from his head, and blew it, tipplety-topplety, to the feet of Father Malachy, who fielded it neatly and returned it politely to the embarrassed ecclesiastic.

"A thousand thanks," came in a well-bred rumble from the clergyman. "A thousand thanks. That wind. Most trying. I'm very much afraid that winds are no respecters of parsons, a-ha."

Now Father Malachy was not used to meeting nice spruce clergymen of the Anglican dispensation and so he stood awkwardly and said nothing; but the other, noting that the rescuer of his top hat also wore a Roman collar, became positively hearty and boomed as though he were preaching over the wireless to unseen millions:

"I see that you also are a parson. How *very* curious."

"I am a Catholic priest," said Father Malachy with humble pride.

A cloud, or rather the shadow of a cloud, passed rapidly over the semi-Grecian features of the Reverend Humphrey Hamilton, Master of Arts of the University of Cambridge; but it was gone almost immediately and the clergyman said with a gracious smile:

"I see." And, nodding across to the dark bulk of the presbytery, added: "Then you are from the other side of the road in more senses than one?"

"Yes and no." Father Malachy smiled. "You see, I am not permanently attached to the parish of Saint Margaret of Scotland. I am a Benedictine monk and I have been loaned by my abbot to Canon Geoghegan in order to instruct the people in the use of plain chant."

"Fine-man-Canon-Geoghegan," the Reverend Humphrey Hamilton said in a quick slurring voice which seemed to imply that, in his opinion, Canon Geoghegan was seventeen kinds of a congenital idiot. And, indeed, his next remark endorsed this semblance of an implication for, without pausing to nod his head in approval of the merits of the canon, he went on: "But, my dear Father—I *may* call you 'Father,' may I not?—surely in these enlightened days plain chant and all that doesn't stand much chance against this sort of thing?" He pointed to the notice board which had broken in upon Father Malachy's meditation. "Surely, my dear Father, in these days when it is so important to get hold of the young people, we must use other and newer methods to compel them to come in? Surely we must bring religion into line with modern thought, must we not?"

It was unfortunate that the Reverend Humphrey Hamilton did not know better the obstinate obscurantism of the monkish mind or he would never, having been educated at Charterhouse and Trinity Hall, have used such an expression as "bring religion into line with modern thought." For monks think, funnily enough, that the Christian religion was true when it was delivered to the Apostles and that therefore it cannot be improved or made more true since truth, like God, is eternal. But the Reverend Humphrey Hamilton, being a well-read man and, so the ecclesiastical reporters said, in the vanguard of contemporary philosophers, did not know this and so he was a little pained and quite surprised when Father Malachy said sternly:

"If you will allow me to say so, sir, I think that your notice board is in the worst possible taste. Further, I think that these 'enlightened' days—as you call them—are most unenlightened and that to talk about bringing religion into line with modern thought is as sensible as talking about bringing impressionism into line with hydraulics."

As has already been pointed out and indeed as has already been observed from his forbearance with Canon Geoghegan, Father Malachy was a mild and gentle man and one of those few Christians who really try to practise that most difficult and trying part of Christianity known as Loving Your Neighbour. It is, therefore, all the more extraordinary that he should have lost his temper with a nice man like the Reverend Humphrey Hamilton merely because that clergyman had expressed an opinion which had already been accepted as a dogma by the broadest-minded stockbrokers and the prettiest young girls of the day. But then, as has been indicated at the beginning of this chapter, Father Malachy was only a poor monk and had passed all his life in a Church which was unenterprising enough to ladle out the same doctrinal broth to broad-minded stockbrokers and pretty girls as to crossing-sweepers and policemen.

However, the Reverend Humphrey Hamilton was very much a man of the world (he used to say "damn" when he missed his drive and, when with check-suited and check-minded laymen, to prefix the adjective "bloody" to the adjective "awful") and so, knowing that he was *à la page* in theology and that Father Malachy wasn't, he said, with infinite charity:

"Come, come, my dear Father. Surely your words are rather hard, are they not? I will ask you to believe me when I tell you that I had no intention of offending you. Indeed, speaking personally, I may say that I have the greatest respect and admiration for members of the Western Church—our Roman Catholic friends, as I never fail to style them when publicly touching upon controversial matters. After all, I was merely trying to make clear to you my point of view. And we are, all of us, entitled to our own convictions, aren't we?"

But Father Malachy, instead of being pacified by the gracious and generous words of the Reverend Humphrey Hamilton, went on being rude:

"Your point of view, sir, reduces to absurdity itself and all other points of view. And when you say that we are, all of us, entitled to our own convictions, you mean that we are entitled to be convinced about anything except that our conviction is exclusively right. Points of view in theology are as idiotic as points of view in mathematics. I am just as entitled to believe that two and two make five as I am to believe that Our Lord could let the world be deceived in essential matters for nearly sixteen hundred years."

His sentences went hurtling at the Reverend Humphrey Hamilton, who was standing with one hand on the top of his silk hat for fear that the wind should again remove it from his head; and the wind, seeing that there was nothing further doing as far as the hat was concerned, took the sentences and blew them apart again into words and sent them flying on to the car lines where, since there was no microphone to hand them on to all stations, they were run over and cut to meaningless syllables by the trams.

"A little *vieux jeu* all that, surely?" said the Reverend Humphrey Hamilton in a less charitable tone than before. "I know that it's quite a literary fashion these days to be mediaeval, but mediaevalism won't wash when it is a question of running banks or making young people worthy fathers and mothers of tomorrow."

Father Malachy was a little taken aback and looked it. He knew nothing about literary fashions and imagined, so ignorant was he in those matters, that Mr. Beverley Nichols was a wholesale dealer in marzipan. He had answered the Reverend Humphrey Hamilton with the arguments he had been taught as a student and he was quite at a loss to understand what the other meant by his talk of running banks and making young people worthy fathers and mothers of tomorrow.

"I was not aware that I was following any fashion, literary or otherwise," he said. "I was merely giving the answer which the Catholic Church has always given to her critics and to would-be reformers throughout the ages. And, as far as I can see, the answer is distinctly unfashionable."

"I am glad," said the Reverend Humphrey Hamilton, with a wispy little smile, "that you are not of those papists who imagine that the novels of Mr. Gilbert Keith Chesterton and the extremely snappy marriages which are celebrated at Brompton Oratory can justify a system of thought and practice which is naturally repugnant to the British mind. No, my dear Father, I am afraid that you and your colleagues will have to think of something better than that." His smile became a grin as he concluded: "And I am also afraid that your worthy Canon Geoghegan is not doing your cause any good by his perpetual fulminations against that excellent little establishment down the road known as the Garden of Eden."

Father Malachy was at a loss what to reply. He did not, as has been told, approve of the canon's attitude towards the Garden of Eden and yet he could not say so to an energetic heretic like the Reverend Humphrey Hamilton for fear that the admission should be misinterpreted as disloyalty.

The Reverend Humphrey Hamilton noted his hesitation and, imagining perhaps that he was on the point of winning a victory for light and reason and common sense, asked:

"Would you care to accompany me for a short way? I have to go and pay a call on the secretary of the Unselfish Society—a most worthy undertaking, I can assure you—and I am afraid that I have not got such a very great deal of time at my disposal. I suggest this because I am finding our discussion quite profitable. Yes, I mean it, quite profitable. These friendly little disagreements do so much to smooth away misunderstanding, do you not think?"

"I will go with you for *two* short ways," said Father Malachy, calling to mind what Our Lord had said about walking miles, lending cloaks, and turning the other cheek.

"Very apt," said the Reverend Humphrey Hamilton, partly because he *did* think it apt, partly to show that he recognized the evangelical counsel which had inspired the remark.

So they set off down the street, the Reverend Humphrey

Hamilton very tall and grand and Father Malachy very small and humble.

"It has always seemed to me," the Reverend Humphrey Hamilton boomed to the city and to the world, "it has always seemed to me that Spain and Portugal furnish the final argument."

"I beg your pardon," said Father Malachy who had been trying so hard to keep pace with his companion that he had heard only an impressive sequence of meaningless rumbles.

The Reverend Humphrey Hamilton, who liked the sentence, re-rumbled:

"It has always seemed to me, it has always seemed to me that Spain and Portugal furnish the final argument."

"You mean?"

"I mean that the bleeding Madonnas, tawdry churches, sanctified amulets, and unshaven clerics to be found in the Iberian Peninsula constitute, to the normal, healthy English mind, the ultimate refutation of the Roman theology." He paused to decide that the phrase was not bad, considering that it had been hatched against the wind, and that it was worthy of inclusion in his next "living religion" sermon. There would be a silence in the church and, grasping his scarf between thumb and forefinger, he would thunder slowly and powerfully across that silence: "The bleeding Madonnas, tawdry churches, sanctified amulets, and unshaven clerics to be found in the Iberian Peninsula constitute, to the normal, healthy English mind, the ultimate refutation of the Roman theology." That "...the ultimate refutation of the Roman theology" was especially good. But what was the poor fish saying? He forced himself to listen.

"I do not see that these things which you mention have anything to do with the matter. You are, like most superficial observers, confounding the unessential with the essential. The Catholic religion is an intellectual religion. We are afraid of nobody on that score. Take Saint Thomas Aquinas, for instance. Take his *Summa.* To anyone who can read Latin there is in that book an answer to every so-called modern problem. People seem to imagine that difficulties and doubts are the discoveries of today. Saint Thomas Aquinas knew them all and answered them all in the twelfth century. As for the exaggerations of the temperamental Latin races, well, they simply don't matter. The true, cold Catholic reality is the thing which matters."

"What about Saint Januarius?" the Reverend Humphrey Hamilton asked gleefully. "What about Saint Januarius? Is that the true, cold Catholic reality? Tell me that. Or is it one of the exaggerations of the temperamental Latin races? Eh, tell me that."

"I do not see why you should deny to Almighty God the power of liquefying at certain seasons the blood of one of His saints. And you must admit that He has been wise enough to locate the miracle in Italy, where Latin logic at once interprets such manifestations as a pulling apart of the curtain to *show* that the Catholic religion *is* true. In these islands such an occurrence would be at once taken as a proof that the Catholic religion was false. The British, for some reason or other, can only accept as true a religion which shows every sign of being false."

"*Very* clever." The Reverend Humphrey Hamilton dragged out the adverb as though it were a piece of elastic. "I must admit that you express yourself well. But why all this insistence on miracles? They are really so very unnecessary and so very impossible. I hope, my dear Father, that you will not think that I am trying to be unkind when I say that the balance of opinion among our most representative scientists is entirely against the possibility of miracles occurring or ever having occurred. Natural laws, my dear Father, are simply not broken."

For fully a minute Father Malachy did not speak, and when he did his voice was trembling with unhappiness.

"And Our Lord's miracles, sir? What about them? Do you believe in them? Do you believe that Our Lord turned water into wine at the marriage feast in Cana of Galilee? Do you believe that He raised up Lazarus from the dead? Do you believe that He Himself rose from the dead and ascended into heaven? Do you believe that He was the Son of God?"

The Reverend Humphrey Hamilton was not an unkind man. He had, it is true, read volumes of anthropology and comparative religion and metaphysics and had quite honestly arrived at the conclusion that the Old and New Testaments were greatly exaggerated accounts of the spiritual history of an obscure and over-imaginative nomadic tribe. But he knew that there were still large numbers of people, less well-read than himself, who believed with all their heart and soul that the traditional Christianity was really and wholly true. So he answered gently:

"My dear Father, you must remember that the Bible narrative has been largely coloured by the Eastern imaginations of those who wrote it and that consequently words and actions which were not His have been attributed to Our Saviour."

Poor Father Malachy became unhappier than ever. Not having read Bertrand Russell and Freud, the Reverend Humphrey Hamilton's words sounded to him blasphemous and sinful and, driven to futility by his spiritual pain, he said weakly:

"I am afraid, sir, that you are not a Christian."

"Not as you interpret the word, perhaps. But if by being a Christian is meant serving others and not self, then I think I may humbly claim the distinction. I do not think that if I say to a mountain 'Be thou removed into the midst of the sea,' the mountain will budge an inch. I do not think so for the very simple reason that it is against the natural law that mountains should, to use the Psalmist's phrase, skip like rams."

Then Father Malachy, in his misery, said a very unkind thing.

"I have always noticed," he said, "that heretics and unbelievers are the first to take credit for observing a commandment so difficult that even the saints of God boggled over it. And, as for what you say about mountains, I am quite convinced that, if God willed, He could cause your church or the Garden of Eden to be transferred into the middle of the Sahara."

The Reverend Humphrey Hamilton was charitable enough to overlook Father Malachy's first sentence and human enough to understand that it had been prompted by great mental agony; but, looking round, he saw that, in the heat of their discussion and in order to let their arms wave support and encouragement to their tongues, they had stopped bang outside the front door of the Garden of Eden, so, confining his charity to Father Malachy's first sentence, he pitched into his second:

"Do you honestly mean to stand there and tell me that, in this twentieth century and in this metropolis of learning, God could perform the miracle of transporting this home of light and healthy amusement through the ether? My dear Father, please reflect upon what you are saying."

Father Malachy turned to gaze upon the institution which had caused Canon Geoghegan such uneasiness. Through a coloured glass door an electric light burned mysteriously, like the far-away sanctuary lamp of an eclectic religion. Perhaps modern young women were even now giving instruction to would-be initiates. Perhaps even at this moment the Bee Bee Bee was having his five shillings' worth. Perhaps anything. And on the outside there was a huge notice, printed in blue and red and, indeed, not unlike that outside the Reverend Humphrey Hamilton's church, which announced that tomorrow night, Saturday, the tenth December, was what was technically known as a late night and that the ladies of the chorus of the *Whose Baby Are You?* company, now playing to crowded houses at the Empire, had, of their graciousness, condescended to be present. Saturday, tenth December. The date, for some reason or other, kept repeating itself in his mind. Tenth December, tenth December, tenth December. And then, in an instant, he remembered. The tenth of December was the feast of the Translation of the Holy House of Loretto. "*Deus, qui Beatae Mariœ Virginis Domum per Incarnati Verbi mysterium misericorditer consecrasti, eamque in sinu Ecclesiae tuae mirabiliter collocasti...*" the collect began.

"O God, who by the mystery of the Word, therein become Incarnate, didst, in Thy mercy, consecrate the House of the Blessed Virgin Mary, and wondrously didst translate it into the bosom of Thy Church…" It was an amazing coincidence that he should be discussing with a heretic the miracle of transportation on the very eve of the festival of the translation of the dwelling-place of Our Lady.

And suddenly, sure that it was more than a coincidence, he was saying:

"Tomorrow is the anniversary of the translation from Nazareth to Loretto of the house in which Our Blessed Lord became incarnate by Our Lady. It is a miracle in which, no doubt, you find yourself unable to believe. But if you will meet me here tomorrow night at half-past eleven o'clock I will, by the help of God, cause to be transported to any place you may mention the Garden of Eden, its late night, and the ladies of the chorus of the *Whose Baby Are You?* company. At eleven-thirty sharp. Don't be late."

And, without another word, he crossed the road and, a huddled little figure in huddled black clothes, disappeared into the presbytery of the Church of Saint Margaret of Scotland.

2.

THE remainder of the morning passed dismally for Father Malachy. He took up the day's issue of a prominent daily, read in gigantic headlines: FIVE NATIONS ARE STRAINING THEIR EVERY NERVE TO WREST FROM BRITAIN HER SPEED SUPREMACY BY LAND, AIR, AND WATER, put it down again and let his cry go up: "How long?" He had just, you see, obtained a glimpse of that darling modern world which delights us all so much and, not understanding the nature of a progress which seemed to lead nowhere, he felt wounded, lonely, and miserable. He himself believed so strongly in Christ and in this life being but the prelude to another and fuller life that his soul was lacerated by the realization that there were others to whom Christ was only rather an uncomfortable Confucius and life but being able to lunch in London and dine and wine in Berlin on the same evening. He had not been educated, as we have been educated, to regard religion as being rather a bad guess at a riddle which nobody can solve, and he was mediaeval enough to regard people who disbelieved in the guess as traitors to Our Lord. Poor little Father Malachy. He sat in his very uncomfortable room with the one million nine hundred and seventy-second copy of a hustling and bustling up-to-date newspaper on his knee and wondered what his holy father Saint Benedict must think about it all.

At lunch he was still wretched and, as he sat down to table with Canon Geoghegan and Fathers Neary and O'Flaherty, he felt that life was indeed a sorry business. Here they were, four papist clergymen in bulging, slovenly, ill-fitting black clothes, sitting down to eat some very assertive haddock, four ecclesiastical knockabouts with the mark of the Holy Ghost upon their souls, four clumping, lumping ineffectives as direct successors of the Apostles in a city which didn't care two straws about their mission. And all around them was unbelief, in the next house, in the next street, unbelief or that dreadful, ill-mannered heresy which had reduced fair Scotland to the level of a second-rate Lancashire. "O dear Jesus," he prayed silently, "You who have been silent so long, give the people a sign that they may know that all this modern intelligence is bunkum."

Father Neary, a small, fair-haired priest with mischievous blue eyes, shouted across the table to Father O'Flaherty, who had red hair and rode a motor bicycle:

"Say, Mike, and phwat will ye be thinking o' the Hibs now?"

And Father O'Flaherty shouted back:

"Faith, Tommy, and I'm thinking that the Hearts will be after beating them."

Canon Geoghegan said nothing, but went on picking at his fish, methodically, earnestly, as though he were disembowelling Immanuel Kant's *Critique of Pure Reason*. To tell the truth, he did not approve of association football any more than he approved of modern dancing; but he realized that, under the existing rules, it was less likely to give rise to immorality, and so he wisely tolerated what he could not suppress. A curious priest, Canon Geoghegan, and one whose mentality differed strangely from that of Father Malachy. Father Malachy accepted revelation as a beautiful poem which was, by the grace of God, true; Canon Geoghegan accepted revelation as a set of facts, as unaesthetic in themselves as Covent Garden in the early morning, which were unfortunately true. Perhaps this little difference of interpretation may account for their not being able to see eye to eye in the matter of the Garden of Eden.

But at the present moment Father Malachy was more in sympathy with the canon than he had ever been before, for he felt that it was most unseemly to talk of football at a moment when Scotland and the world were careering off to eternal damnation through heresy and unbelief.

"I met the clergyman of the church opposite while I was out this morning," he began by way of bringing the conversation round to the heavenly athletics.

"Sure and ye nivver did," said Father Neary through a mouth crammed with potatoes, bread, and fish. "Not ould Humphles, the ould Judas. Sure and ye nivver did."

"The dirty, lying ould scallywaganorum," said Father O'Flaherty. "And if I was his mother, I'd be after taking down his holy pants, that I'd be, him and his disbelaiving in Jaysus Christ."

Canon Geoghegan munched on for a few seconds in silence. He disliked what he described to other Irish ecclesiastics born in Midlothian as "the loathsome effervescences of the untutored Erse" and had had more than once to reprove his curates for using uncouth language from the pulpit. For sometimes a real Rolls-Royce would pull up outside the Church of Saint Margaret of Scotland and some bewhiskered and be-spatted duke, accompanied by daughters well dressed enough to look sinful, would ascend the long flight of steps and penetrate into what was, for nine dukes out of ten, the House of Rimmon. And on such occasions it was unfortunate if the Reverend Michael O'Flaherty, priest forever after the Order of Melchisedech, were to take the opportunity of telling the congregation that they were a "lot of lazy, half-baked spalpeens with divil a thought for the darlin' Lord Jaysus in the Most Holy Sacrament of the Altar, begob." That sort of thing didn't go down with dukes who, between a flutter at Deauville and a win at Newmarket, carried the canopy when archbishops were consecrated. And Benedictine monks, pest take them, were almost always as grand gentlemen as the most worldly dukes and could discuss, with equal ease, fishing in the Hebrides or the invalidity of Anglican Orders. He munched on, therefore, just to show these two young scallywags from County Down that he, Shamus Canon Geoghegan, was annoyed with them.

And when at last he spoke he did so in a thin trickle of quasi-donnish sarcasm.

"You are referring, I presume, to the incumbent of the pagoda on the other side of the road?"

"Precisely." Father Malachy began to speak quickly because he wanted to lighten his trouble by passing part of it on to others. "I was walking outside his pagoda, as you so aptly call it, when he came out of the west door and a gust of wind blew his hat from his head and rolled it along to my feet. I picked it up, naturally, and handed it to him. He thanked me and we began to talk theology. In the course of our conversation I learned that he did not believe in miracles or in such well-established doctrines as the Resurrection of Our Lord Jesus Christ."

"The blaspheemious bletherskite!" said the Reverend Father Neary.

"The holy, stinkin' heretic!" said the Reverend Father O'Flaherty.

Canon Geoghegan, who was sitting at the top of the table, inclined his head to left and to right just as though he were in the middle of the *confiteor.*

"Please," he said in a tone which completely turned his request into a command and, addressing himself to Father Malachy, continued: "The phenomenon, my dear Father, is by no means so unusual as you seem to imagine. The pernicious work begun at the Reformation bears fruit ever more and more abundantly. Heresy always breeds heresy. Protestants began by denying Purgatory and the Mass and they are finishing by denying the Virgin Birth, the Divinity of Our Lord, and everything which makes Christianity a religion. Yes, I think that we may fairly say that they have reduced Christianity from the level of a supernatural religion to that of a philosophical opinion which, like opinions on all other matters from toffee-making to road-mending, may be right and may be wrong." He paused to allow his phrase to sink into the minds of his hearers. "Mr. Humphrey Hamilton is only one of many, my dear Father, and his convictions, or rather his *un*convictions, are shared by all clergymen popular and prominent enough to be asked to write for the Sunday newspapers on Mixed Bathing, Marriage, or the Spiritual Aspect of Face Cream." The canon snorted. "And yet some people wonder why monks and nuns shut themselves off from the world."

"But how very terrible," said Father Malachy, whose misery had been increased rather than decreased by the canon's words. "And Mr. Hamilton told me that he was of the opinion that the Scriptures were in many respects inaccurate."

"Shakes," said Father Neary, "but foine I'd loike to dot him one on the boko."

The canon again inclined his head disapprovingly in the direction of Father Neary.

"I presume," he said dryly, "that he told you that they had been largely coloured by the hyper-Orientalism of the writers."

"Curiously enough, such were almost his very words."

"It is not so very curious, my dear Father, when one reflects that for the past ten years leading novelists, who have never read the Bible since they were expelled from one of those Public Schools which have made England what she is, have been telling us Sunday by Sunday that anthropology and geology have clearly shown that the Bible is a sentimental best-seller which contrived to get itself written only because the Children of Israel never played rugby football." He glanced at both his curates as though to say: "There is not, my friends, any difference, *sub specie æternitatis,* between association and rugby," and wound up: "The phenomenon of disbelief, my dear Father, may be described as a sort of intellectual German measles from which it takes three centuries, instead of three weeks, to recover."

One part of Father Malachy's soul felt happier and one part felt more wretched. He was happy to hear Canon Geoghegan dispose of heresy in such quick, competent phrases and he was wretched because the fact that it could be so easily disposed of seemed to argue that he had been somewhat rash in undertaking to transport, by his own volition and the help of the Trinity, the Garden of Eden to any place which the Reverend Humphrey Hamilton should name.

"I am afraid that I have been rather rash," he said shyly. "You see, I was so shocked and pained to discover that the truths of our holy religion were regarded with such contempt by professedly intelligent men."

The canon looked inquiringly at Father Malachy.

"I do hope that you weren't rude to him, Father," he said. "Mr. Hamilton can be rather an awkward neighbour when he likes."

"Rude?" Father Malachy shook his head. "No, Canon, I wasn't rude. We got on to talking about the blood of Saint Januarius and moving mountains into the middle of the sea, and he was so emphatic in his assertion that miracles were, and had always been, impossible that I undertook, with the help of God and His holy Mother, to transport, tomorrow night at half-past eleven o'clock, the Garden of Eden to any part of the universe which the reverend gentleman should name."

At this statement even the Reverend Fathers Neary and O'Flaherty became solemn and Canon Geoghegan left off altogether picking at his fish and, placing his knife and fork with French irregularity upon his plate, said quietly:

"I am afraid, Father, that I don't quite understand. Would you mind repeating the last part of your sentence."

Father Malachy repeated:

"I undertook, with the help of God and His holy Mother, to transport, tomorrow night at half-past eleven o'clock, the Garden of Eden to any part of the universe which the reverend gentleman should name."

"My *dear* Father! Do I understand you to say that you have entered into a wager with this very unreasonable schismatic and heretic to duplicate the miracle of the Flying House of Loretto? Do I understand you to say that?"

Father Malachy nodded.

"You've got the idea," he said. "Only the contract is in no sense of the word a wager, as no money is to change hands. I merely wish to vindicate the miracles of antiquity by performing, through God, another one on Saturday night. And it was precisely the fact that tomorrow, the tenth of December, is the Commemoration of the Translation of the Holy House of Loretto which inspired me to challenge him."

"'Inspired,' my dear Father, is a strong word and, in this instance, I fear that it is also a wrong word." The canon's face, ordinarily a hearty crimson, was a pale and disapproving purple. "If you will pardon my saying so, I think that you have been most foolhardy and have exposed to considerable ridicule the cause which we all have so much at heart."

"Sure," said Father Neary, "and miracles are intoirely out of fashion these days. If one were to take place in his lordship the bishop's bedroom the right riverend ould gint would be after hushing the indaicency up."

"I agree," said Canon Geoghegan. "And what is more, I am sure that the united hierarchies of Scotland, Ireland, England, and Wales would be of the same opinion."

But the disapproval of Canon Geoghegan and Father Neary had only the effect of making Father Malachy more determined than ever to carry out his project. Gone were the wretchedness and the hesitation of a few minutes ago and in their place came a firm purpose to carry out the undertaking and, with the supernatural to crown the natural, to succeed. If good, sound priests like Canon Geoghegan were against miracles, then there was more need than ever to vindicate them.

"Perhaps," he said gently, "you had better send a telegram to His Holiness informing him that Father Malachy Murdoch, of the Order of Saint Benedict, intends, with God's grace, to confound unbelievers by publicly performing a miracle at half-past eleven on Saturday night." Perceiving that his words had gone home, he continued, still more gently: "If you will examine the secret places of your hearts, reverend Fathers, I think you will find that it is lack of faith which is at the root of your objection to my proposed course of action. In other words, you are afraid that I won't bring the trick off and that my failure will confound the believers and not the unbelievers. And yet, reverend Fathers, morning after morning, each of you stands at God's altar and, by virtue of the priesthood in him, performs the most wonderful marvel of all: the transubstantiation of bread and wine into the Body and Blood of Our Lord and Saviour Jesus Christ. That marvel, I admit, cannot, by its very nature, be exposed to crude physical tests; but it is nonetheless a marvel for all that and it is performed three hundred thousand times each day, in obscure Spanish village churches just as certainly as in metropolitan cathedrals. Surely, in view of the wonderful way in which that marvel never fails, it is not too much to hope that Almighty God will enable me to perform the very much less striking miracle of transporting through the air a dancing hall which, on your own authority, Canon, has caused a great deal of scandal in this parish?"

A silence fell over the room, a silence through which the clanging of the trams outside was heard and was not heard. The three secular priests looked at one another uncomfortably and looked away again as soon as their eyes met. Each recognized the logic in Father Malachy's argument and yet each felt that the transportation through the air of the Garden of Eden was a miracle which not even the Pope and all his College of Cardinals could perform.

"My dear Father Malachy," the canon began slowly, "I should be the last to deny the existence of the supernatural. I am a Catholic priest and I know my theology too well to be guilty of any leanings towards modernism. But the marvel of Our Lord's birth each day in the Mass, my dear Father, is a marvel which He Himself guaranteed when, in an upper room with His apostles, He Himself said the first Mass and pronounced, for all the centuries to hear, the first 'HOC EST ENIM CORPUS MEUM.' We have no such guarantee that *your* miracle will come off. Indeed, we must take it from the very fact that there are such things as natural laws that Almighty God is very unwilling to break them."

Father Malachy thought over the canon's words before he replied to them.

"I quite see the point that you have just made, Canon," he said. "We have, of course, Our Lord's promise that He will come and come again amongst us in the Blessed Sacrament of His Love and we have no promise, not even a hint from a very minor saint, that the Garden of Eden will take the air on Saturday night. The Mass, of course, is what one might call a natural supernatural occurrence. That is to say that Our Lord's promise has made it quite certain that each time a validly ordained priest pronounces the words of consecration over bread and wine they will become, transubstantially and in an unseen but real manner, His Body and Blood. The transformation is as inevitable as the law of gravity and so we may say, in very truth, that the Mass is an integral part of the heavenly mechanics. Of course, heretics and unbelievers, who accept only the evidence of their senses, argue that, because the Bread still appears to be bread and the Wine to be wine, there has been no marvel. Now, reverend Fathers, the words 'heretics' and 'unbelievers' are used by us so hardly that we sometimes forget that Almighty God loves them just as much as He loves us and that He wishes to garner them all into that eternal barn which we call heaven. And one of His chief means of converting heretics and unbelievers is by the use of spectacular miracles, the reality of which nobody can deny. Our Lord's resurrection and ascension and the descent of the Holy Ghost upon the Apostles are among such spectacular miracles as are also the miracles effected by the Apostles and by their successors. Sacred tradition is full of the accounts of such spectacular miracles, about which we may observe two things: firstly, that they were almost invariably used to induce or to strengthen faith; and, secondly, that they occur more and more rarely as time goes on. The second fact we, who are of the household of the Faith, may interpret as a sign that, as the Gospel became more widely spread, God considered that there was less need for spectacular miracles. But the Church has never lost the power to 'do signs and wonders in His Name' and, as a proof of this, we have the cures at Lourdes and little local miracles like the liquefaction on the nineteenth of September in Naples of the blood of Saint Januarius. And in countries like China to which the Faith has been given only in comparatively recent years miracles, if we are to believe the missionaries, are of quite frequent occurrence. The position, then, would seem to be this: that God, of His infinite mercy, yields for a short time to the human misstatement that seeing is believing and then, when Faith has been firmly established, gradually turns the tap off, although He always lets fall a dribble or two out of compassion for a wicked and adulterous generation. At least, reverend Fathers, that is the light in which the matter appears to me."

"Very well put, Father," said Canon Geoghegan. "But we in Scotland have had the Faith for years."

"My dear Canon Geoghegan," Father Malachy answered as patiently as the grace of God allowed him to, "I am afraid that you have got things upside down, haven't you? We in Scotland have *not* had the Faith for years; we have lost it for years, which is a very different thing. A mere handful, it is true, have kept the Faith and there are, thank God, a few places in the Western Highlands where the sanctuary lamp was not extinguished by the Reformation. But what of those who are inoculated with the errors of Knox and Luther and Calvin? What of the millions who have never heard of the Blessed Sacrament? Go along Princes Street and ask the first man you meet what he understands by the term 'the Catholic Church' and see what sort of answer you get. And add to these millions in Scotland those others and many more millions in England and America and then perhaps you will realize that there is quite a need for some supernatural fireworks to bring the English-speaking peoples back to God. You, Canon, are a priest as I am and you must realize just as clearly as I do that the only solution of all our modern problems and difficulties is to be found in the submission of the entire world to Christ's Holy Catholic Church."

"*Touché*," the canon admitted as gracefully as he could, mangling rather than pronouncing the Gallicism. "We are indeed, as you hint, a benighted country and we need nothing so much as a thorough dosing with Catholic doctrine. Everywhere men are seeking religion with some authority behind it and a Church which is international rather than national and sound rules by which to conduct their lives, and everywhere they are too blind to see that what they seek is seeking them. And so the Church of God is made to seem a sect among the sects and superior persons who inhabit the west end of Edinburgh and the east end of instruction regard us as being a perversion of that which they themselves have perverted. And the intellectuals, the pseudo-psychologists and the twenty-four handicap metaphysicians! Only this morning I was reading an essay in which, a man who ought to know better said that man created God in his own image and that, as there were many kinds of men upon the earth, *quot homines, tot dei.* Aphrodite and Our Blessed Lady were, according to this seer, two different names for two different psychological states. And the harm that such stuff works." The canon jerked his head backwards towards the window through which the world, a pale grey humming reality, could be faintly discerned and more faintly heard. "Indeed, Father, I do not think that it is any exaggeration to say that the predominance of such pernicious philosophies has been responsible for the springing up all over our beloved land of institutions like the Garden of Eden where sin is but a pleasant sensual titivation set to music. You are quite right, my dear Father; we have lost the Faith for years."

Father Malachy saw his opportunity and snatched at it. He knew, of course, that the Middle Ages, when novelists who thought aloud in Sunday newspapers would have been burned at the stake, had had institutions like the Garden of Eden and some which had been ever more startling, but he did not take the trouble to point this out to Canon Geoghegan and prayed that, on the Last Day, Our Lord would overlook His omission in view of the supernatural end for which it was made.

"Therefore, Canon, you are bound to admit that now is the time to strike. One little spectacular miracle and we shall prove to the world, in a manner so sure as to be irrefutable, that we have the Light and the Truth and are the divinely appointed guardians of the Way. One little spectacular miracle," he wheedled, "and we shall be able to go and teach, not only Scotland, but all nations with the certainty that they will listen to us."

The canon thought away and away behind the *ego* that was Shamus Canon Geoghegan. He desired, since he was a priest and a good one, the peace of Christ in the reign of Christ just as earnestly as did Father Malachy and he was weary of a city and a world which regarded his religion as a picturesque survival from an uneducated age. Yes, perhaps the time was indeed ripe. Perhaps, too, God was intending to use Father Malachy in a sphere other and higher than that of instructing working men and boys in the glories of plain chant. God had used so many humble, unlikely people that you never knew whom He was going to use next. Bernadette and the pale, sickly Thérèse of Lisieux, Jean Vianney who had been such a dolt that his bishop wasn't keen on ordaining him. Why not, then, Father Malachy? And it would be a wonderful thing for the parish to have the Garden of Eden transported to the North Pole.

"Perhaps you are right, Father," he said uncertainly and seemed to be looking for words with which to build and brick a sentence which should adequately express what he was feeling in the privacy of his soul.

"I *know* I am right," said Father Malachy. "You see, it wasn't I who made that contract with Mr. Hamilton; it was the Holy Ghost."

At these words both Father Neary and Father O'Flaherty became quite white and frightened and Canon Geoghegan, returning to pick at his fish which was now quite cold, could only murmur a half-hearted caution:

"All right. But not a word to the bishop, mind. He mightn't like it."

And, feeling that they were nearer to that reality which they preached than they had ever been before, the four priests finished in silence their rather uninteresting Friday luncheon.

CHAPTER V

1.

NEXT morning at nine o'clock, Father Malachy, wearing the Eucharistic vestments of the Catholic Church, made his way to the foot of the high altar and, pushing back his amice from his head, began the service known to three hundred million Christians as the Sacrifice of the Mass.

Now Father Malachy believed, as every true priest must believe, that he was, for the moment, the representative of Christ and that into the white wafer of bread and welling up within the chalice of wine would come, as he bent to pronounce the holy words, the Body and Blood and Soul of Him Whom he represented. He believed this because the Church told him that this was so and because he realized that, with the wonders of the sun and moon and stars and seasons about him, there was no reason to doubt that Our Lord kept coming among us in this very sweet and lovely manner. And so, unlike some priests who gabble their way through the most beautiful poem and the most beautiful reality which the world has ever known, he pronounced slowly the darling Latin and crossed himself as though he were tracing upon his soul the agony of Our Saviour's passion and death and moved through the whole glorious mystery with the reverence and the dignity of a boy who had been ordained the day before and with the lingering affection of a holy old man who must die that night.

In the nave two broken-down old women watched him with tenderness in their eyes. They lived, those two broken-down old women, by scrubbing floors and they had, each of them, a husband who drank and daughters whose profession was that of Saint Mary Magdalene before she poured the precious ointment upon the feet of Our Lord. Two broken-down old women, all chilblains and rheumatism and teeth that weren't there, two broken-down old women, illiterate and all the rest of it, who stood, such is the topsy-turviness of the heavenly economy, a very good chance of one day occupying the front row of the stalls with Saint Catherine of Sienna and Saint Francis of Assisi.

But Father Malachy, who kept the custody of his eyes each time that he turned to give a *Dominus vobiscum,* was as unaware of their presence as he was of the chartered accountants who, bristling with income-tax repayment forms and balance sheets and all the other high intellectual paraphernalia which have made their calling the noble thing it is, were hastening to their offices within an eternity and five minutes of the altar at which he was celebrating.

Outside the trams, red, lusty, and agnostic, clanged by. Outside the great kaleidoscope kept turning and men and women, with bowler hats and powder puffs and Pekinese dogs to hide their immortal souls, went solemnly about their important unimportances. Outside Edinburgh continued to be bleak, Protestant, and to lead countries which had never heard of it in science, philosophy, medicine, and respectability. But inside the Church of Saint Margaret of Scotland, perched like a supernatural toad between a music hall and a doubtful lodging house, Father Malachy stood at the altar of God and traced once more the epic of Our Lord's Crucifixion. To the left he moved, to the centre and to the right, and always slowly and gently as though his feet would do penance for the helter-skelter of modern men. And back to the centre again and on into the deep sea of the Mass where, with Peter and Paul, Simon and Thaddeus, Cosmas and Damian like rocks about him, he bent and brought God to bread amid an unheard fluttering of unseen wings.

2.

THAT same night at half-past six Andrew Gillespie, the Bishop's Bad Brother, leaned across the counter of a very popular bar near the Waverley Steps.

"Winnie," he said to the young lady on the other side, "what's on at the Garden tonight?"

Winnie, who was a pretty young girl with the same philosophical outlook as the Dean of Saint Paul's, smiled a smile which contributors to popular magazines would describe as "displaying two pearly rows of even, white teeth."

"Eh don't kneow, Mr. Gillespie," she answered in the dreadful English affected by Edinburgh young ladies who wish to appear more *de famille* than they really are. "But they say that the chirus from the Aimpire is geowing to be thaire and that it's a lit night."

"A late night, is it?" The Bee Bee Bee nodded his head in that slow up-and-down manner which, because the deliberateness of the nodding suggests that the nodder is reviewing the whole range of the higher mathematics and physics, has won for Caledonians the reputation of being one hundred times as intelligent as they really are. (A Scotsman nods his head for the same reason as a puppy chases its tail and, expressed in terms of pure thought, the nodding equals the chasing.) "A late night, is it?" he asked again, returning from the higher mathematics and physics which he hadn't visited. "Och, well, Ah s'pose Ah'd be'er dander along. The bit lass'll be pleased tae see me."

His last sentence was almost inaudible, partly because he spoke in that thick, guttural tone which prideful Picts imagine to be as attractive as the Irish brogue and which, in reality, resembles nothing so much as a horse with a cold in the head, partly because the bar was crowded with young gentlemen in chatty golfing suits who were discussing loudly what various teams had been doing with various sorts of balls during the afternoon. But the Bee Bee Bee didn't care. He spoke as much for the benefit of his own soul as for Winnie's; and, if Winnie didn't hear, his own soul did, down beneath the padding of his woolly waistcoat. So he said it again, this time for the exclusive benefit of his own soul (Winnie was now up at the other end of the bar serving a purple-faced stockbroker): "The bit lass'll be pleased tae see me."

His soul and the bar kept getting more golden and glorious and jolly. Indeed, as the gin and Italian vermouth dissolved into vapour inside him, he found it increasingly difficult to tell which was his soul and which was the bar, so much at one with these hearty, healthy, friendly men did he seem. For the Bee Bee Bee was a low-brow, not of the aggressive my-boy-is-a-duffer-at-Greek-but-by-Gad-he-plays-for-his-school type, but of the genial beery brand whose critics say, according as charity gives them utterance, that they are "dull but good-hearted" or "good-hearted but dull." And all around him were low-brows: golfing low-brows, footballing low-brows, low-brows who liked to watch other low-brows footballing, biscuit-making low-brows, all the great plus-foured mindless who, getting their names in the papers only when they were hatched, matched, or despatched, did more to mould contemporary Caledonian thought than all the professors, authors, and bigwigs that the country had ever produced. He himself belonged to the second hierarchy of Caledonian low-brows, to those who wore a mental kilt and were all for Rabbie Burns whom they never read and for the Church of Scotland which they never attended; but he bore no ill-will to his superiors of the first hierarchy who preferred, or had had preferred for them, Kipling and the nice clean white surplices of what was known by those Scots who didn't belong to it as the English Church. For, among low-brows of the first hierarchy or among low-brows of the second hierarchy, he was among his ain folk, among the noble army of average men who, by their common sense and breadth of vision, had raised profound thinkers like Vilma Banky and Warwick Deeping to the platform from which, nobody saying them nay, they dispensed their sooth to a world which had poisoned Socrates and burned Savonarola. So his soul, surrounded by other souls with the same image and superscription upon them, expanded, like a balloon into which gas is pumped, into a golden orb of sleek content.

"Aye," he said again, "the bit lass will be pleased tae see me." The words were uttered to nobody in particular, as Winnie was still serving the purple-faced stockbroker, but they spiralled up nonetheless surely into the haze of alcohol and tobacco and passed with them into the great limbo of things said, smelt, and tasted. And as they swung upwards they were heard by a lanky egg merchant who had just finished his second.

"Wimmen," said the egg merchant sententiously and rolling the word round his mouth as though it were a cough lozenge, "wimmen are fair hellish."

The Bee Bee Bee turned and nodded his head quite seven times before he replied.

"Aye, laddie. But there's wimmen and wimmen, mind. Aye, there's wimmen and wimmen." His eyes moistened ginnishly as he thought of Bubbles and her golden hair and of how she snuggled up to him in taxicabs. "Aye, there's wimmen and wimmen, mind. And mine's as bonny a wee bit hen as ever cried cock-a-doodle-doo."

"But hens don't cry cock-a-doodle-doo," said the egg merchant, who, *de par sa profession,* knew something about the matter. "Hens don't cry cock-a-doodle-doo. Cocks, old man, cocks. You've got the blanket the wrong way up."

The Bee Bee Bee laughed noisily.

"Good for you, Jock," he said. "Hens don't cry cock-a-doodle-doo. Anyway, ye ken what Ah mean. Ah've got a dandy wee bit lassie and no mistake. She teaches dancing down by at the Garden of Eden."

"Is that a fact?" said the egg merchant.

"Yes. And Ah've just been asking Winnie here what's on down by tonight and she tells me that there's going to be fine high caryings-on. A late night, you know, and all the lassies from the Empire waggling their wee bit beam-ends. Ah wouldn't miss it for worlds. Bubbles—that's my lassie's name—doesn't expect me, but Ah'm thinking that Ah'll just be giving her a surprise." The alcohol he had consumed and the general brotherly atmosphere common to all bars made him feel that the egg merchant was a man in whom confidences could be safely deposed. "Ah may be on the wrong side of forty, but Ah've got young ideas." He laughed as though the phrase and the feeling were original. "Yes, Ah've got young ideas all right."

The egg merchant, his whisky lapping in a yellow tide up the side of his glass, leaned nearer.

"Nice piece, is she?" he asked, with a look which showed that he was fully prepared to take a vicarious pleasure in her niceness and in her piece-ness.

The Bee Bee Bee winked cheerfully.

"I should say that she is. She's only twenty and she has got legs with muscles like a racing champion's. All yon dancing, Ah s'pose."

The egg merchant rolled his eyes lugubriously.

"Aye, all yon dancing, as you say." He stared across at the tiers of bottles on their shelves as though reading on the labels of the Erastian Johnny Walkers and the Ultramontane Benedictines the foretelling of a doom yet to come. "As you say, all yon dancing." His eyes gradually lost their Calvinistic gloom and he continued briskly and with every appearance of taking pleasure in what he was saying: "Ah hope Ah'm not offending you, mister, but perhaps a word in season mightn't do any harm. Mind you, no offense meant. But seeing as you and me are standing here pally like and talking away as if we'd known each other all our lives and seeing as you have honoured me with your confidence Ah might as well tell yew that in my opinion all yon dancing is dee-moralizing and is making the lassies o' Bonnie Scotland no better than a lot o' koantanental baggages. Mind you, Ah'm no a great boy for the kirk, but there's something in what the meenisters say about dancing turning little white vurgins into scarlet primer donners. And it's not just hearsay, mind yew. Ah kent a bit of goods in Glasgow..."

The Bee Bee Bee said with what he imagined to be simple dignity:

"Scarlet primer donners be damned. Ma wee Bubbles is as innocent as the sunlight on her hair. As innocent as the sunlight on her hair, Ah tell you."

The egg merchant took a gulp at his whisky and continued lusciously:

"Aye, they're all as innocent as the sunlight on their hair until they're caught napping." He nodded with the aggravating self-assurance of a man who knows human frailty too well ever to do business or make love on trust. "As Ah was saying, Ah kent a bit of goods in Glasgow. Proper little pink-and-white angel she was, and to look at her you would have said that butter wouldn't melt in her mouth. Real pally with a friend of mine in the motor trade, she was. Said she loved him and all the usual yarn. Loved him!" He laughed loudly and harshly. "Perhaps she did. But she loved his money more. And one day he found out that she'd been up to all sorts of high jinks with medical students when he wasn't there. He was a middle-aged gentleman like yourself."

His last sentence discomfited the Bee Bee Bee who, being a neat and pseudo-military forty-five, did not like to be termed "middle-aged."

"Ah'm on the wrong side of forty," he admitted again, but heavily this time and despondently as though it were another ten years that he was acknowledging. "But that's not middle-aged."

The egg merchant, who was a youthful thirty-eight, emptied his glass.

"The half of three-score years and ten is thirty-five," he said maliciously. "And yewth to yewth, that's the trewth. Lassies are all very well and patting a pair of young knees does us old lads good. Makes us younger than we are and more sympathetic to the clarion call of Progress," he declaimed, misquoting the leading article in the current issue of his favourite technical journal. "Ah, well, must love you and leave you, Ah s'pose. The missus, you know. Doesn't like to be kept waiting. So long, old scout. No harm meant. Liked the looks of you and just thought Ah'd like to tip you the wink. Cheerio!"

And with a wave of the hand he allowed himself to be caught into the whirlpool of the swing door and was whisked into the Leith tram and non-existence.

3.

The Bee Bee Bee was a simple soul who lived, as do many souls less simple than he, as though his sense perceptions were the only realities and as though armchairs and pork pies and pretty girls were exclusively and finally armchairs, pork pies, and pretty girls. For him science and her mysteries were as uninteresting and as unintelligible as theology and her mysteries, and the tremendous implication of electrons dancing within the illusion called matter left him as unmoved as the equally tremendous implication of angels dancing on the point of the combination of illusions called a needle. He lived, therefore, the inconsistent life which the men and women around him lived: he believed, or said that he believed, or allowed it to be said that he believed, that this world was a school for eternity and he lived just as though he were persuaded that when you were dead you were very, very dead, and he was among the first to laugh at those who deprived themselves of pleasures here below so that they might find a more lasting habitation beyond the grave. Like most of his kind, he would have scorned the name of mystic even if he had known precisely what it meant. And yet that was what he was: a mystic, an inverted mystic who found in beer and dancing instructresses what tired businessmen found in golf, and worldly young women in love-making, and monks and nuns in prayer and contemplation: an escape from his own personality or rather a taking of it and plunging it in something bigger than and exterior to itself. For, from Saint John of the Cross to Miss Gertie Gitana, we are all of us, hypodermically or hyper-psychically, transcendentalists; and Andrew Gillespie, leather merchant and hedonish, was, pathologically, a great deal nearer to the Right Reverend Monsignor Robert Gillespie, Bishop of the Catholic Church and repressionist, than either he or the bishop realized.

Miserably, mechanically, feeling that the egg merchant's remarks had called in question the security of one of the two great sources of his spiritual ecstasy, the Bee Bee Bee clamped half a crown on the counter and wandered out and along the corridor to the grill room of the North British Station Hotel which, like the bar, was full of beefy young men discussing rugby, golf, cricket (in Australia), fornication (in Paris) and aëronautics. Miserably, mechanically, he sat down and ordered a mixed grill, a bottle of Guinness and a Welsh rarebit to follow and, closing his mind to and annihilating the beefy young men around him just as successfully as Father Malachy had, a month or so previously, closed his mind to and annihilated the crowds in Queen Street Station, Glasgow, he called up before him, radiant in her confinement with himself, Bubbles whom he loved and who said, laughingly and with a wind in her words, that she loved him, Peggy McNab of number two-hundred-and-something Crosscausswayside; and, so real was her presence in his mind and so perfectly did he re-fashion and create her from the threads of his memory, he annihilated not only the beefy young men around him, but also the mixed grill, the bottle of Guinness, the Welsh rarebit when it followed and the humble, pathetic little waitress who served them.

Peggy McNab. He remembered the night that he had first met her and the way that she had laughed, all down in her tummy and up in her eyes, when he had called her "Ma bonny wee hen" and, when the dimming of the lights for a tango had made him bolder, "Ma ain wee bluebell." So slim had she looked and so proud in her black silk frock and so very much the lady that he had hesitated, primed though he was, to present himself at the pen where she sat with others less fair than herself and ask her for "this one, please." But when he had seen young man after young man and elderly man after elderly man come up and claim her with a brief question and had seen her give a nod of her head and rise and sail away, golden hair, black frock, slim pride and all, in their embrace, he had hesitated less and less and finally had gone as the others had gone and had taken her in his arms, an impersonal loveliness rented at sixpence per five minutes.

At first he had not dared to converse with her, but had contented himself with the feel of her at the points of his fingers; but the warmness of her flesh and her so-near-and-yet-so-far-ness had made his contact with her, due only to the fact that he had sixpences and that she wanted them, seem of such little value that he had, at the finish of his fourth consecutive dance, invited her to the upper balcony where they had drunk lemonade and exchanged the awkward remarks that are always exchanged between two people who desire to be friendly and who have not as yet sufficient knowledge of each other's souls to make good conversation or good silence. Cigarettes, however, had succeeded where lemonade had failed, for, after a few and unscientific puffs, she had, tapping her forefinger against the thick butt of Messrs. Abdulla's Number Eleven, flicked onto the carpet a thin powder of ash. "Ash is good for carpets," she had smiled, remarking that his eyebrows were lifted in mock censure. "Yes," he had agreed, "when it's not your own carpet." At which sally they had both laughed just as though it had never been made before and when, five minutes later, they had both agreed that summer was warmer than winter they were well on the way to their subsequent romance and bi-weekly lunches at the North British Station Hotel.

Yes, he thought, he had sat at this very table with her and, oblivious of the prosperous lawyers and stockbrokers around them, told her that she was his puir wee doo and she, as fundamentally Caledonian as himself, had wriggled with pleasure from hat to shoes and had said that she might be puir and she might be wee, but that she didn't like doos, who were the saftest o' the burrds, and that she preferred, when all was said and done, to be his puir wee hen. Yes, at this table which, with its vacant place opposite and its bottle of Worcester sauce like a gloomy steeple, looked as though it had never seen her and the gold of her and the teeth of her when she laughed. But it had, though, and it had seen her twenty times if it had seen her once, now in pale green, now in a flaming scarlet business, now in black. And, closing his eyes, it seemed to him that she was there now, laughing to his laugh, preedling to his preedle, answering "Sugar Daddy" to his "Bubbles." The ghost of her, perhaps, just as there were ghosts of her in the woods at Roslyn and on the sands at North Berwick and in a wee bit bunker on the golf course at Gullane. Hundreds of ghosts of her who should return—who knew?—until the end of time to tables and Worcester sauce bottles and woods and sands and bunkers just as, on nights when nobody was looking, a ghostly Mary, Queen of Scots, was rowed, by ghostly oarsmen in a ghostly boat, across the black and silent waters of Loch Leven.

He opened his eyes. No, she was not there, not a suggestion of her, not a ghost of a ghost. Perhaps he was just a foolish elderly man and perhaps, as that fellow in the bar had hinted, wimmen were fair hellish and perhaps, when he wasn't there, she carried on with young fellows and let them kiss her. Perhaps even she laughed at him behind his back and imitated, to more competent lovers, his billing and cooing. Perhaps he was, to her, just a well tailored free lunch. But no, she had said that she loved him and that he was ever so much nicer than a lot of silly boys who were always wanting this and wanting that. She had said that several times and she had said it as though she had meant it. Perhaps he ought to have asked her to marry him and have freed her from the necessity of having to earn her living by dancing, night after night, in the arms of a succession of potentially amorous young men. Perhaps...

His mind, dazed with imaginings to which it was unaccustomed, refused to conjecture any more; and he determined that that night he would go early to the Garden of Eden and would ask Miss Peggy McNab his bride and his bonnie to be.

4.

THEY were dancing a tango when he arrived and the red and yellow lights which ordinarily lit the polished arena were lowered to a dull, indeterminate purple. Pish-pish, shish-pish, pish-pish whispered the feet of the dancers as, half-closing their eyes and looking as languorous as their blood and their upbringing would allow them, they did their best to appear, according as they were male or female, like Mexican lads of the village holding broadminded women of the world or like broadminded women of the world being held by Mexican lads of the village, pish-pish, shish-pish, pish-pish; and the music, a dreamy wail suggestive of practical ungodliness beneath orange trees, ta-a-a-a-a, ta-la-la-la-la-la-ta-la-la-la-a-a-a-a, it went, and ta-a-a-a-a, ta-la-ta-la-la-la-la-la-la-a-a-a again.

He looked, as he entered, in the pen on the left; but there was nobody there except a pale and rather unattractive instructress who was reading, as best she could in the insufficient light, a paper edition of the late Miss Marie Corelli's *Temporal Power.* He moved, therefore, across the strand of crimson carpet which led to the edge of the dancing floor and, after darting his eyes in between and around the Mexican lads of the village and the broadminded women of the world, caught sight of her moving her body in slow and apparently rapturous harmony with that of a tall young man who was holding her slightly away from him and was gazing down upon her upturned face as though he read there the assurance that she was quite willing to be his baby and anything else that contemporary erotics demanded. She was, as usual, in black and the silk seemed to swirl out from her and back to her all the more sweetly because it was not he who piloted her; and her hair, always golden, was now a great torturing sun which he would never see again. He saw her and, seeing her, he saw her all the times that he had ever seen her and as he had never seen her before. Pish-pish, shish-pish, pish-pish went her feet and ta-a-a-a-a, ta-la-la-la-ta-la-la-la-la-a-a-a-a went the music and, as she glided around and away from him, the nights in which he had walked with her seemed to glide away too and his heart felt sicker and wearier than it had ever felt before.

But when the dance was over and she saw him standing there she left her partner and came running to meet him, all flying skirts and smiles.

"Sugar Daddy!" she exclaimed, holding out both her hands to him. "This *is* a surprise."

He wanted, of course, to smile back and to hail her with the same cordiality as that with which she had hailed him; but Satan, dressed as an egg merchant, stood behind him and whispered that wimmen were fair hellish and that she had seemed to be enjoying her bit caper with that laddie, hadn't she now?

"Who was that young squib?" he asked.

She rounded her eyes to two great orbs of inquiry.

"What young squib, Sugar Daddy?"

"That young la-di-da loon you were dancing with just now?"

"Oh, him." She jerked her head backwards. "Oh, yon's just one of those lounge lizards. All feet and no head, you know." She noticed the unhappy expression on his face and, puzzled by it, asked: "Why, what's the matter, Sugar Daddy? You've not been going and getting jealous, have you?"

"Ah..." But how could he explain about that skinny-malink in the bar without appearing foolish and unnecessarily suspicious? How could he explain having trusted her all these months and then, because of a few words from a man whom he had never seen before and would never see again, beginning to doubt her? Of course, it was that remark about his being middle-aged that had done it. Yes, of course, but he could never explain that to Bubbles. Besides, it might make her think him older than he actually was. "Ah..." he said again and stood looking like an overgrown schoolboy who has forgotten the piece of poetry which he is supposed to have learnt by heart.

But Peggy McNab was a young woman who combined will power with tact.

"Well," she said, "perhaps you'll tell me when we're nice and cozy upstairs, Sugar Daddy." She put her arm in his and began to propel him, prancingly, towards the pay desk. "So you can just buy me out for ten dances, Sugar Daddy, and come with me like a good boy and tell your Bubbles what's biting you. That'll cost you five bob, Sugar Daddy, and it's cheap at the price. So run along and pay up like a man."

He went to the cash desk and asked, with heavy self-consciousness, the girl who presided at it for ten dances, please. A button was pressed and, ting, ten rectangles of pink cardboard came sliding out of a silver canal. "Tain. That'll be faive shillings, please, Mr. Gilaispie," said the girl, who knew him. "Faive shillings, please. Paig's in luck tonight, and no mistake."

It had never previously occurred to him that dancing instructresses could have too much dancing, but the girl's remark opened his eyes to the possibility that his Bubbles might get as tired of dancing as he himself of buying and selling leather. And the valedictions of her companions, who were waiting behind the barrier for some Saturday night Juan to look with favour upon them, made the possibility seem more probable. "Cheerio, Paig," they sang in ragged anthem. "If you can't be good be careful and think of us still shaking a leg while you're playing at being well-off up there."

But he had not time to meditate upon this new revelation, for Peggy took him firmly by the arm and marched him upstairs to what was known as the "sit-ootery" and, pulling him onto a sofa uncomfortable enough to be moral, went straight to the point.

"Spit it out, Sugar Daddy," she said. "What's the little black beast on your back? Come on, now. There's nothing whatever to be afraid of. I'm all ears and noses. 'Specially noses, Sugar Daddy."

"Ah..." Once more he was tossing on waves of inarticulation, once more the words refused to come. And she was looking so sweet, too, with that perky wee look in her eye, just like a saucy bit sparrow asking for bread. He was a great big stookie, that was what he was. Only a great big stookie would have had ideas about such a lassie as Bubbles carrying on behind his back. Why, Auld Nick himself would have seen that the lassie was as straight as a long drink of water. Yon yellow yite in the bar. He'd like, by heavens, to have the baisting of him. He'd kick him all the way from the Barclay Church to Ferguson and Forrester's. He'd... But there was Bubbles, the wee soul, waiting for an answer. "Ah..." he said again and stuck again.

"Yes?"

Cripes, but the lass really looked as though she meant to get the truth out of him.

"Ah was just wondering if you still loved me, Bubbles," he evaded unconvincingly.

"That's a lie, Sugar Daddy. You know perfectly well that I love you and that I'll always love you. The truth, please."

There was nothing for it. Slowly and with many incoherencies he told her the truth: how that he had been having a wee hoot in Winnie's bar and how that he had got into conversation with a blether there and how that the blether had blethered that wimmen were fair hellish and that dancing instructresses carried on behind their middle-aged admirers' backs and how that seeing her dancing with that all-dressed-up-and-no-where-to-go young swanker had made it seem that the blether had been right and that wimmen were just a lot of worthless besoms. And then, the difficult part over, he became more fluent and told her that he was very sorry for being so silly and asked her to forgive him and, as a sign of her forgiveness, to marry him. "You see how it is, Bubbles?" he concluded. "Ah'm just so much in love with you that I can't bear to go on living without you."

Peggy did not immediately reply. She sat and stared, or rather she sat and did not stare ahead, for the conventional declaration seemed to her as golden and shining as a new line of poetry uttered for the first time. And as she sat there the past few years came chasing back along the lanes of her memory. There had been good times and there had been bad times, but chiefly bad times, for it is not easy for a girl to live by dancing alone; and what with boys wanting to take her for runs in motor cars and elderly moochers imagining that just because she was an instructress they could do what they liked she had had her work cut out. Of course, there had been decent men, heaps of them; but none had been so decent as this funny, woolly, silly old Sugar Daddy of hers who loved her for herself and who had just asked her to marry him. No, she was not sorry that this dancing business was all over. And she would just love being married and having pink, squiggly babies.

"You're a daft cookie, Sugar Daddy," she said when she had swallowed some of her emotion. "A daft cookie." She tapped her forefinger three or four times on her forehead. "Quite balmy."

"How daft?" he asked, afraid that she was rejecting him.

"Oh, just daft, Sugar Daddy," she answered and laid her head as nearly on his shoulder as the etiquette of the establishment permitted. But from the tone of her voice and from the way that she came as near to him as she could he realized that she was his to marry; and from the sigh that he gave and the way that his hand made for her shoulder and then drew back she knew that he knew what embarrassment had prevented her from putting into words. For quite half an hour they sat there with the lemonade untouched on the table in front of them and with their hearts going pit-a-pat, pit-a-pat deep down within them. Pish-pish, shish-pish, pish-pish went the feet of the dancers below them, pish-pish, shish-pish, pish-pish, rather like the waves of an invisible sea creeping up a phantom beach. Now it was a tango, now it was a foxtrot, now it was a waltz; but the procession of events below meant no more to them than the contemporary *status quo* of French politics. For they loved mutually and knew that they loved mutually and were tasting one of the two great ecstasies as yet undamaged by a hyper-mechanized civilization.

It was twenty minutes past eleven when he spoke.

"Let's get out of here, lassie. Let's get a taxi and drive to the Back of Beyond."

"I'm with you every time, Sugar Daddy," she said. "But don't forget that you'll have to pay for the rest of my dances."

So once more he had to present himself at the cash desk and once more he had to receive, in exchange for a number of sixpences, an equal number of rectangles of pink cardboard. And when he had pocketed them and fetched his hat and coat and when Bubbles, all powdered and fluffed, had descended from a mysterious privacy it was twenty-eight minutes past eleven and the chorus ladies from the *Whose Baby Are You?* company had arrived and, in purples and greens and yellows and slim, tantalizing scarlet, were moving round the floor with deliberate, feline grace, like free-thinking tigresses self-consciously having a night out.

"Get me a taxi," said the Bee Bee Bee to a uniformed boy, who immediately vanished through the whirling glass door.

5.

FROM six o'clock to nine o'clock Father Malachy, with the purple stole of penance about his neck, had sat in the confessional and listened to those who came to tell him their sins and had forgiven them in the name of our Lord Who said to His apostles: "*Quorum remiseritis peccata, remittuntur eis; et quorum retinueritis, retenta sunt.*"† From Leith Walk and the High Street, from Morningside and the respectable parts of Murrayfield they had come to be shriven and to rise

† "Whose sins ye shall forgive, they are forgiven them; and whose sins ye shall retain, they are retained."

up from their sins and to lead lives more worthy of Him Who died for them on Calvary: young women who had gazed too long in the looking-glass, old women in shawls who had thrown plates at their husbands, young men who had lusted after women in their hearts, old men who had found it difficult to supernaturalize their charity, potential saints and actual sinners, high and low, rich and poor, all God's children without wings. And to each of them, after the tale had been told and the pardon asked and the amendment promised, had come the voice of Father Malachy, borne through the grille on the breath of the Holy Ghost: "*Ego te absolvo a peccatis tuis in Nomine Patris et Filii et Spiritus Sancti*"[†]; and to each of them, as their sins fell from them and were washed away in the great stream of dead longings and hated loves and burned-out passions, had stolen down the peace of Christ, a stalactite of compassion to their stalagmite of contrition.

And in the other three confessionals Canon Geoghegan and Father Neary and Father O'Flaherty had also been giving a rub to their portion of the hebdomadal laundering. "My son, you're hanging over hell fire by a thread," Father Neary had roared to a fishmonger's assistant who had passed a rather too undenominational weekend at Dunoon and "I take a very serious view of your case," Canon Geoghegan had minced to a university lecturer in Spanish who, from motives of intellectual pride, had given the Sacraments the go-by for eighteen months; but to both the fishmonger's assistant and the university lecturer in Spanish had come the same sweet absolution and Father Neary and Canon Geoghegan, wiping, like barbers cleaning razors in between customers, the sins which they had just heard from their minds, had turned to greet and to bless the next penitent and to apply to his soul, in virtue of their priesthood, the mystic Lysol which, so antiseptic were its fumes, cleansed and healed almost before it had been put on.

† "I absolve thee from thy sins in the name of the Father and of the Son and of the Holy Ghost."

But that had finished two hours ago and as the last absolved sinner, his soul glowing like a newly polished frying pan beneath his waistcoat, had left the church they had all of them come out of their confessionals and, after a brief prayer to Our Lord cradled in Bread on the high altar, had passed through the sacristy to the clergy house where they had sat down to their Saturday night supper of Cambridge sausages and tea. The meal had been a silent one and not, as happened when Fathers Neary and O'Flaherty were in good spirits, a noisy recapitulation of the day's association football exploits. For the fact that one of their number had contracted to bring off a miracle that night depressed rather than exhilarated them and the Worcester sauce with which the Reverend Father Neary had liberally seasoned his sausages tasted, as the seasoner afterwards remarked to the Reverend Father O'Flaherty, "like mucky wather from a mangy ould Prothestant drain, begorra." It was not that they did not believe in miracles (to have heard Father O'Flaherty on the *Lives of the Saints* would have startled the Pope); it was rather that they felt that Almighty God was a bit economic with miracles these days and that, if He were prevailed upon to modify His policy, it would not be to play swallows and eagles with semi-unrighteous dancing halls. Indeed so silent were they all that, as soon as the last drop of tea had chased the last bit of sausage into the last sacerdotal belly, they had all gone upstairs to their bedrooms where they remained until eleven o'clock when they met again by appointment in the dining room.

Father Malachy was the last to arrive. He was rubbing his hands vigorously as he entered and his eyes were twinkling with that merriment which seems, here below, to have been reserved for those who are fools for Christ's sake.

"Well, reverend Fathers," he greeted, "it's a cold night for a miracle."

The other priests, who were standing in an irregular semicircle on the far side of the table, looked at one another with quick, slanting glances and Canon Geoghegan cleared his throat and delivered a little speech which he had obviously prepared for the occasion:

"My dear Father," he said, "I do not think that there is any need to tell you that, during your brief stay with us, you have endeared yourself to us by your charity, by your wisdom and, above all, by your great love for Our Blessed Lord. We have all of us—I speak, my dear Father, for Father Neary and for Father O'Flaherty as well as for myself—we have all of us come to look upon you as a real friend because a true friend, and as an ideal priest because a true priest. But we think—again I speak for Father Neary and for Father O'Flaherty as well as for myself—we think that you may have been led by an excess of zeal into this contract which is the cause of our meeting here tonight. Please, Father, try not to misunderstand what I am saying. Believe me, I am speaking from a deep affection for the truths of our holy religion and not from any desire to hurt you or to retard the work of God. Briefly, what I want to say is this: if you feel, my dear Father, that you *have* been over-zealous and that you are asking rather a lot of Almighty God in demanding this particular miracle at this particular time, then we will undertake to see Mr. Humphrey Hamilton on your behalf and to inform him that—the phrase, Father, is Father Neary's, not mine—the miracle has been scratched; but if you still persist that you are acting under the Divine Guidance, then we shall be only too willing to do anything in our power which may aid you to carry out what would be a great vindication of the supernatural and the removal of a great spiritual stumbling-block from the parish of Saint Margaret of Scotland."

Father Malachy's eyes became damp with feeling as he listened to Canon Geoghegan's words, for he realized that they were prompted, not by any ca' canny mammonishness, but by a real love for the truth and dignity of religion.

"Shall we sit down, reverend Fathers?" he asked. "We look so like a lot of parsons in a worldly drawing room when we are standing up like this. All smiles for the hostess, you know, but wishing that her daughter would not put quite so much paint on her face." And, when they were seated round the table at which they had so recently eaten, he continued: "Reverend Fathers, I cannot thank you enough for the very kind words which your hearts have spoken to me through the mouth of Canon Geoghegan. It is very pleasing for an old man who must soon go to meet his Lord to know that his last few deeds and words on earth have been pleasing to the most worthy of his fellow men. And for your offer to arrange matters for me with Mr. Humphrey Hamilton I must also thank you, because I know that it was made in a kind and generous spirit. For that offer, reverend Fathers, I must thank you, I say, but I must not accept it. I want you to trust me"—he looked quickly back at the clock—"for twenty-five more minutes. Twenty-five more minutes, reverend Fathers, and I think that each of you will realize that, in this little matter of the translation of the Garden of Eden, I have been walking by a faith so certain that it has almost been knowledge."

Once again the three secular priests glanced unhappily at one another. Miracles were their everyday business or rather—which was not quite the same thing—the *raison d'être* of their everyday business. They believed that Jesus Christ had been born of the Virgin Mary by the Holy Ghost, which was a miracle; they believed that He had risen from the dead and ascended into heaven, which was another miracle; they believed that the Holy Ghost had descended upon the Apostles and, pouring out from their hands, had consecrated bishops and priests right down the centuries, which was a succession of miracles; they believed that Our Blessed Lady had appeared to certain privileged saints and that, to this very day, miracles by healing were performed by her intercession at Lourdes. But, in spite of the fact that their whole religion was based upon and permeated with the supernatural, they felt that it really would be a little bit too much of a good thing if the Garden of Eden were suddenly to dissociate itself from God's ordinary laws of conservation and start flying through the air like a super-zeppelin. Their hesitation expressed itself momentarily upon their eyes and then passed back into the secret places of their souls; for they had given their word to Father Malachy that, if it still seemed to him that he must attempt his miracle, they would help him to the utmost of their capabilities.

"I must thank you, Father, for so finely interpreting our feelings in this matter," said Canon Geoghegan. "And, now, I don't think that there remains anything to be said except to tell you once more that we are all at your disposition and shall be willing to undertake any tasks which you may assign to us."

"But I haven't any tasks to assign to anybody," Father Malachy exclaimed. "The Garden of Eden is going to fly by the grace of God. I shan't require anyone to stand by and blow if the miracle doesn't come off." His quick mind perceived that his confidence was serving only to make the others more uneasy than they already were, so he ceased to banter and continued gravely: "Reverend Fathers, I can see that you are still unconvinced. I am sorry because I know that my power over words is so slight that I shall not be able to displace that unconviction by conviction. But I would, for your own peace of mind, ask you to remember that all that I am going to do is to ask Almighty God to superimpose one miracle on top of another. We all of us know that God's Will is always actively employed in conserving the universe and that the fact that no inanimate object can move without being moved by some natural agency is just as much one of God's miracles as if all the dancing halls in the world were suddenly to be levitated into the air and never to come down again. And remember, I beg of you, that we know literally nothing about the real form of matter. Matter, reverend Fathers, is anything but what our senses tell us that it is. Matter is all electrons just as the Host consecrated at Mass is all God and we know no more about the motion of electrons in the one than we know about the motion of God in the Other. Please, reverend Fathers, try to show a little more confidence in my inspiration than I would in yours if our positions were suddenly to be reversed." He laughed, half at his own sally, half because he was feeling so very serious. "Twenty minutes more, reverend Fathers, and we'll all be cock-a-hoop singing the *Te Deum* in front of the high altar." He laughed again, but this time in a far-away manner, as though the joke were between himself and God. "Which reminds me that I *have* got a job for one of you. I should be grateful, Canon, if you would send either Father Neary or Father O'Flaherty into the sacristy to lay out the white vestments for a solemn *Te Deum* and to light the six liturgical candles on the high altar."

Canon Geoghegan turned at once to Father Neary.

"Father, will you kindly do as Father Malachy has suggested?" He waited until Father Neary, after an unhappy grimace at Father O'Flaherty, had left the room. "Well, that accounts for one of us. What about the other two?"

Father Malachy appeared to consider before replying.

"Perhaps you, Canon, will be good enough to accompany me. Yes, on the whole, I think that I should feel happier if you were with me. Father O'Flaherty can wait here and watch from the window."

"And sacramentals?" The canon was businesslike. "Holy water and a hyssop, I mean. You'll need those if you are going to asperge the building. And a stole, of course."

Father Malachy shook his head.

"No, Canon, I shan't need anything like that. I shall go just as I am. No, on second thought, I shall put on my hat and coat, as it is a cold night. And now, Canon, as it is a quarter past eleven I think that we had better be going. I should like, if possible, to arrive before Mr. Humphrey Hamilton."

6.

OUTSIDE the night was all black and silver, like a pall over the bier of the faithful departed. The simile occurred to Father Malachy as soon as the front door had closed behind them and he murmured, of his charity, a short prayer for all the poor down-and-outs in Christ. But, by the time that he had uttered "*requiem aeternam dona eis, Domine,*" he was already, with Canon Geoghegan, who was smelling slightly from the brandy which he had just taken to steady his nerves, at the edge of the pavement and he had to give his whole mind to the practical problem of dodging the trams which, like lighted galleons of an anachronous armada, were sailing swiftly up and down the street.

They found, when they had crossed to the other side, a whole rank of motor cars parked with their back wheels in the gutter and their noses pointing with mute optimism towards the presbytery of the Church of Saint Margaret of Scotland. Morris (Oxford and Cowley), Citroën, Rover, Vauxhall, Singer, Daimler, they were all there, the Minerva lying down with the Ford and the Baby Austin sticking her snout in the Hispano Suiza's exhaust.

"Like the green bay tree," Canon Geoghegan anathematized as, two dumpy little figures in black, they began to move along the file of municipally numbered sterns. "And yet, in another place, the Psalmist says that he has been young and is now old and yet never saw he the righteous forsaken nor his children begging their bread. All that I can say is that he must have had an extra fine lunch the day that he trotted out that verse. For my own part, I think that the verse about the ungodly flourishing like the green bay tree is finer poetry and sounder philosophy. The owners of these cars did not come by them by frequenting the sacraments and they are certainly not using them tonight for the greater glory of God."

His words, borne on a little private wind, came unpleasantly to Father Malachy's ears. Surely, he thought and tried to keep himself from thinking, this was not a time to be imputing motives to people whose good faith or bad faith was known only to God. But he said nothing and kept on walking with short, sure steps towards the lighted entrance of the Garden of Eden which was a conglomeration of gorgeous splotches of red, purple and yellow. And as they kept on walking, the one loving and the other hating, they were joined by the Reverend Humphrey Hamilton who looked, in his magnificent top hat, like one having authority and cultured in all English Literature from *Beowulf* to *If Winter Comes.*

"Good evening, gentlemen," he greeted in his rich, broadminded voice. "I see that you believe in arriving in time. Well, well, trains and miracles wait for no man, do they? And my dear friend the Canon, too. I do hope that none of my good parishioners see me for, if they did, they might imagine that I was on the point of going over to the Church of Rome."

"Yes," said Canon Geoghegan, who hated Mr. Humphrey Hamilton as far as was not inconsistent with the divine precept. "And yet neither your parishioners nor mine would imagine, from seeing us in your company, that we were going over to the Church of England. Isn't that, my dear sir, rather a warming thought for a cold Saturday night in early December?"

"*Very* neat," said the Reverend Humphrey Hamilton who, having left a glowing fireside, a glass of toddy, and a book by Mr. J. Middleton Murry in order to witness what he was persuaded would be a dud miracle, was not feeling in the best of tempers. "And yet if I were to be seen coming out of a side street in which there was a house of ill-fame and a theosophical bookshop it would be presumed by all who met me that it was the former establishment which I had been patronizing."

But, before Canon Geoghegan could think of an acerbity with which to cap the Reverend Humphrey Hamilton's, Father Malachy intervened.

"Please," he begged in a tone so earnest that the two disputants immediately felt ashamed of themselves. "We may differ in doctrine, but surely this wrangling must sound very disagreeable to Our Blessed Lord Whose servants we all profess to be."

Now when Father Malachy pronounced the Sacred Name he did not, like many priests, articulate It as though It were "Ramsey MacDonald"; but he spoke It slowly and reverently so that the syllables seemed to be printed before the eyes in scarlet and gold, as indeed they are in illuminated mediaeval missals. And Canon Geoghegan and the Reverend Humphrey Hamilton, hearing him, knew, each in his own way, that here was a man to whom the practise of religion was as important as the theory. They were silent, therefore; and even when three very unspiritual-looking young women got out of a taxi and ran, all legs and laughter, into the Garden of Eden, Canon Geoghegan forebore to make the criticism which he imagined that Saint Paul would have made and tried instead to see them as their Lord Who died for them must see them: as charming silly-billies who found it difficult to watch with Him for one hour.

"We have still another five minutes to wait," said Father Malachy when they halted outside the main entrance to the Garden of Eden. "It is, of course, possible that Almighty God would effect the miracle now if I were to ask Him nicely; but as I can see no purpose beyond our own personal comfort in doing so I think that I had better not. For all we know He may have some special grace to grant in Australia at this moment and it would be impolitic, in view of the nature of my request, to disturb Him before the hour agreed upon. In any case, Mr. Humphrey Hamilton has not indicated to me the place to which he would wish the Garden of Eden to be transferred."

"My dear Father, I *wish* to have the Garden of Eden transferred to nowhere. It is you who wish to have it transferred to somewhere in order that you may convince me that miracles are as possible in the present as they are supposed to have been in the past. I remember, however, that in your challenge to me you stipulated that I should choose the place; and as, in this case as in that of Saint Denis carrying his head, '*la distance n'y fait rien; c'est le premier pas qui coûte,*' I challenge you to transfer this building which we see in front of us to the top of the Bass Rock which lies, as we all know, in the Firth of Forth and slightly to the northeast of North Berwick."

Canon Geoghegan frowned inwardly as he heard the Reverend Humphrey Hamilton's challenge because the Bass Rock, although inhabited only by a lighthouse-keeper and his family, was in the diocese of Midlothian and he would have much preferred the Garden of Eden, if a-flying it would go, to make a thorough job of it and settle down on some desert *in partibus infidelium*; but he recognized that any suggestion on his part was out of the question and prayed to God that he would hear the prayer of His servant Malachy and cleanse the parish of Saint Margaret of Scotland from an establishment which hindered the sanctification of souls.

"Right," said Father Malachy. "The Bass Rock it shall be." He pulled out his watch, glanced at it, put it back again. "And as it is now twenty-seven minutes past I think I shall, with your permission, begin to recite the preliminary prayers. At half-past exactly I think that you will both of you be rewarded for your patience."

And with these words Father Malachy took off his hat and handed it to Canon Geoghegan and bowed his grey head in great and silent prayer. He did not see the few late couples passing up the steps of the Garden of Eden any more than he saw the curiosity with which they turned round to look at the unusual spectacle of three clergymen standing reverently on the pavement outside. He did not see the boy in uniform come tearing out and rush off up the street whistling for a taxi which wasn't there. He did not see and did not hear the trams as, all unconscious of the mystery which was then being hatched, they came clanging up from Leith and went clanging down into Leith. He did not see and he did not hear because his mind was shut to God and because he was praying that He would, of His infinite mercy, grant this little sign and wonder that men might again come to believe in Him and in the truths which He had revealed to them. Through Jesus, by Mary, by Michael, by John the Baptist, by Peter and Paul he prayed, through them and by them and round them and over them to God; and at half-past eleven precisely the Garden of Eden stirred on its foundations, heaved tremendously, rose slowly and surely into the air and was absorbed by the night into a cluster of coloured lights which disappeared rapidly in the direction of North Berwick.

"*Gloria Patri, et Filio, et Spiritui Sancto,*" murmured Father Malachy when he opened his eyes and saw what had happened.

"*Sicut erat in principio, et nunc, et semper, et in sæcula sæculorum. Amen,*" answered Canon Geoghegan, seizing Father Malachy by the arm and rushing across the street to the presbytery before the policeman on point duty could arrest them.

7.

TEN minutes later three figures in shimmering white made their way to the altar of an empty church lit only by six tall candles. "*Te Deum Laudamus,*" intoned Father Malachy, and Father O'Flaherty, invisible in the organ loft, pulled out the stops and let her rip. "*...te Dominum confitemur,*" took up Canon Geoghegan and Father Neary. "*Te æternum Patrem, omnis terra veneratur. Tibi omnes Angeli, tibi coeli, et universæ potestates; Tibi Cherubim et Seraphim, incessabili voce proclamant: Sanctus, sanctus, sanctus, Dominus Deus Sabaoth.*"

On it went, the glorious canticle of Ambrose and Augustine, louder and louder it grew, the heavenly thunder of sheer praise, louder and louder until it seemed that the whole church must burst from matter into sound and go soaring to join the hymns which angels sang round the Throne of God, louder and louder until the praise quietened to prayer and the three priests dropped to their knees in humble commemoration of the Redemption of men by Jesus Christ. And then, rising, they sang to God that He might save His people and that they, who had trusted in Him, should not be confounded forever.

And when it was all over the three figures in shimmering white went as silently as they had come and the candles were put out and the church became again a huge darkness lighted by a single ruby lamp.

CHAPTER VI

1.

AT a quarter to ten on Monday morning Father Malachy, having said Mass at nine, sat down to breakfast (Canon Geoghegan and Fathers Neary and O'Flaherty, having said the earlier Masses, had already breakfasted) and, mindful of the example of Saint Aloysius and the game of billiards, turned a natural operation into a supernatural one by buttering his bread to the glory of the Father and stirring his tea to the glory of the Son and nicking the top off his egg to the glory of the Holy Ghost. But, try as he would, he could not think as exclusively of heavenly things as he wanted because the events of the last thirty-four hours and a quarter kept switching in upon his consciousness and so, excusing himself on the ground that his intention was meritorious and that the earthly matters exercising his attention were as other-worldly as it was possible for them to be, he gave up the exclusively heavenly as a bad job and allowed his thoughts to follow his inclinations.

And, indeed, it was no wonder that he indulged himself in this manner because the miracle, which had begun by being a personal affair between himself and God, had ended by becoming everybody's business. It appeared that an attendant of the Garden of Eden had been the first to notice that anything out of the ordinary had occurred. He had been sent, so he had told the policeman on point duty, by a patron of the establishment at twenty-six or twenty-seven minutes past eleven to get a taxicab and, returning at twenty-five minutes to twelve with one of Mr. Dan. T. Munro's brightest and reddest, he had found a great square hole in the ground where the Garden of Eden used to be. It had taken him quite three minutes to realize that the Garden of Eden had actually been bodily removed from its customary location and another five to persuade the taxi driver that he hadn't been "trying to take a loan of him," so that it had been seventeen minutes to twelve before he had informed the policeman of the mysterious disappearance; and the policeman had quite naturally said "Awa' and tell that to the marines" and "Havers, man" several times before consenting to accompany the boy and the taxi driver to the spot from which they said that the Garden of Eden had disappeared. Then, after a few slow nods of the head and a "Weel, weel" or two, the representative of the law had pulled a notebook from his hip pocket and proceeded to ask those heavy, practical questions which Caledonian constables always ask when something has happened to upset the public order. "Was ye sure ye was inside when the gentleman sent ye outside for to get a taxi?" And what would the gentleman be like? Young or old, fair or dark? Oh, and he was with a lady, was he? Would she be a real lady or—or yin o' yon? And when he got outside, did he notice any suspeecious folk loitering about? Any folk that might be anarchists or communionists or likely to have a bomb on them? So he had noticed three clairgies, had he? Looking as holy as though they were praying at a Band o' Hope meeting. Weel, weel, it couldna be the clairgies now, could it? Did he no mind of seeing somebody mair—mair seenister than a clairgie or a meenister?

By this time, however, quite a crowd had collected and everyone familiar with the district agreed that the Garden of Eden had disappeared and that, all things considered, it was a mighty queer kind of flitting for folks to make. Some remembered having seen it the day before, some that morning and some as recently as an hour previously, and some, whom the policeman had later described as "a lot o' claverin' sweetie wives," said that they had seen lights flying through the air above the London Road and three topers, who had been leaning against the closed door of the public house on the other side of the street, swore that they had seen all the windows of the Garden of Eden go bang up into the sky like the scenery in a pantomime, but had concluded, not unnaturally, that the vision had been inspired by their last "double." Several, however, testified to seeing three clairgies or three meenisters "standing as though they were praying like" outside the Garden of Eden, and a free-thinking soldier on leave from Redford Barracks said that, in his opinion, the clairgies had looked "awfy like as though they were Roamin' Catholickies" and so the policeman, followed by an ever-increasing crowd, had been forced to cross the street and ring the bell of the presbytery of the Church of Saint Margaret of Scotland. And he had had to ring not once but many times because the servants were all asleep on the fourth floor and because the priests had not yet returned from singing the solemn *Te Deum* in church. At last, however, the bell had been heard and Canon Geoghegan, who had expected something of the sort, had restrained Father Malachy from opening the door and they had all gone up to the spare bedroom on the first floor and Father Neary, hugely enjoying the fun, had raised the window sash and asked the policeman below what he wanted. "It's about the Garden of Eden," the policeman had said. "It seems to have fleed awa' and this laddie here says that he saw three clairgies standing outside it just before it got lost. I was wondering if you gentlemen knew anything about it." "Yes," Father Malachy had answered, pulling Father Neary back from the window, "we know all about it. At half-past eleven tonight I, Malachy Murdoch, monk and priest of the Order of Saint Benedict, caused, by the power of God, the Garden of Eden to be transported through the air to the Bass Rock." "Michty me," the constable had exclaimed, "and what for did ye do a thing like yon?" "To show the people that God is still as powerful as He was and that Christ is King of this world as well as of the next," Father Malachy had replied, and a youthful heretic had begun to whistle the tune of a song of which the words ought to have been: "When it's Dimanche in Deauville it's Sunday over here."

By this time the crowd had grown immense as it was being continually added to by contingents from the other crowd which had now gathered round the site of the Garden of Eden. The policeman, unsupported by another of his kind, had been at a loss what to do and had hesitated as to whether to arrest the self-confessed miracle-monger and haul him off to jail. But, as Canon Geoghegan had pointed out, there was no law on the statute book forbidding the performance of miracles and, as the government of the country believed, officially at any rate, in a miraculous religion, he might seriously prejudice his chances of promotion if he were to arrest a priest for carrying out the precepts of their Lord and Master. He had contented himself, therefore, with taking down the names of the clergy resident in the house and with wagging his head and saying: "Weel, this is a fine to-do and no mistake."

All night long the crowds had surged and resurged and all night long there had been catcalls and tugs at the presbytery bell and blasphemies and blessings; and, at seven o'clock in the morning, when Canon Geoghegan had entered the sanctuary to say the first Mass, the church had been filled with a congregation which was not entirely Catholic, Roman, and Apostolic. At this Mass, as at all others, Father Malachy had preached. "My friends," he had said, wrapping himself up in his black habit, "I want you all to join with me in giving thanks to Almighty God for having vouchsafed, through my unworthy hands, to effect a great miracle. Last night at half-past eleven, in order to confound a Protestant clergyman who said that miracles were impossible, I transferred, by the power of God, the dancing hall known as the Garden of Eden from its customary site to the top of the Bass Rock. There is, I am glad to say, no doubt as to the authenticity of the miracle: you have only to look for yourselves if, indeed, you have not done so already; and we were informed early this morning by telephone from North Berwick that the Garden of Eden alighted on the Bass Rock at thirteen minutes to twelve last night. Now, brethren, I want you to do three things. Firstly, as I have already said, I want you to thank Almighty God for having given us and the whole world such a very evident proof of the truths of our holy religion. Secondly, I want you to refrain from vain boasting either among yourselves or in the presence of your non-Catholic friends and to remember that Almighty God has granted this miracle to quicken our faith and not to provide a vulgar sensation. Thirdly, as his lordship the bishop is at present away administering the Sacrament of Confirmation in Cowdenbeath, I want you to understand that my words to you this morning must not be interpreted as the official opinion of the Catholic Church regarding this latest wonder of God, but simply as an exhortation to prayer and humility. A blessing, my very dear brethren, which I wish you in the Name of the Father, and of the Son, and of the Holy Ghost. Amen." At all Masses, including his own, he had preached this short sermon and again at Benediction in the evening.

But unfortunately Father Malachy had been able to preach only to the good Catholics of Edinburgh and to those comparatively few "not of this fold" who came desiring to hear some new thing. He had not been able to preach to the rest of the city, to the grinning stockbrokers who had given up their Sunday golf to come and hum and haw their opinion of the miracle over the great square hole which marked the former site of the Garden of Eden, to the loud-voiced utilitarians from Glasgow who came in their plus-fours and two-seaters to see and to misunderstand, to the trilling young girls who went motoring down to North Berwick to see the Garden of Eden perched lugubriously on top of the Bass Rock; and still less had he been able to preach to the greater public, to Leeds and Manchester and London, to Paris and New York and Madrid, to the thousand and one places to which the miracle was broadcast. To them he had trusted that the miracle would preach for itself and that the spiritually indifferent the world over would be brought to the feet of Christ by this very wonderful supernatural happening. For surely, he had argued, when those who had despised religion as superstition heard of this vindication of the miraculous, all that they could possibly do would be to kneel in the dust and ask God to forgive them for their past unbelief.

Edinburgh, however, was by no means willing to accept the miracle as genuine. For more than three hundred years Edinburgh had known that Roman Catholics were not to be trusted and that they paid their priests for licenses to eat meat on Fridays and to rape the daughters of good-living Presbyterians. Edinburgh was not to be taken in by any of that popish hanky-panky. That sort of thing was all very well for Italian ice-cream merchants and temperamental South African operatic tenors, but it cut no ice where Edinburgh was concerned. The miracle was no miracle at all; it was just auto-suggestion or mass-hypnotism or sheer fraud. As one devout old lady remarked to another devout old lady in front of the scene of the miracle: "Thae Catholics is wrang, Jeannie; and even if they prove they're right they're wrang." Against the logic of such illogic even the gates of heaven could not prevail.

And what had been true of Edinburgh had also been true of the Great Big World where leading cinema actresses and dubious deans oiled the wheels of international thought. The ordinary editions of the Sunday newspapers, having been printed on the evening on which the miracle had taken place, had contained no echo of the unusual happenings by the Firth of Forth but had been the customary hash of dramatic criticism, novel reviews, murders, adulteries and epoch-making articles on modern girls and their attitude towards the Athanasian Creed. As soon, however, as the first news had got to London every editor worth his blue pencil had rushed to press a special edition in which the circumstances of the "alleged miracle" were chronicled in the most purple journalese and in which the "leading thinkers of the day" stated their views on what it was impossible for them to have any views at all. There had been totally inaccurate descriptions of Father Malachy and the Reverend Humphrey Hamilton and wireless-transmitted photographs of the chorus of the *Whose Baby Are You?* company being rescued from the Bass Rock by the North Berwick lifeboat crew; and Miss Puggie de la Warrene, America's leading *prima ballerina* then appearing in London, had stated that seeing was believing as far as she was concerned and the most dubious and most metropolitan of the deans, interviewed through a closed bathroom door, had said that, in his opinion, miracles were as bad form as they were bad science and that he thanked the innate sanity of the English people that no Anglican clergyman would have been allowed to perform one. Even the saner journals, those literate publications in which real thinkers write for thinkers, had been most guarded in their references to the matter. "Miracle is as far from our metaphysic as Edinburgh is from London," one cautious critic had written, "and we would advise our readers to await further details from the North before concluding that the natural laws are no more legal than they are natural but mere physical conventions which may be overthrown at any moment by the caprice of a discredited tribal god."

Such had been the reasonings and unreasonings of those not of the household of the Faith.

Catholics, who are generally supposed to swallow without difficulty weeping Madonnas and other knotty parts of the heavenly tapioca, had, as far as could be ascertained, been unwilling to commit themselves to belief or to disbelief in the miracle. At any rate, those in high places had been as ca' canny as a batch of Auld Kirk elders sniffing at a doubtful haggis. "Whether or not this miracle said to have been performed in Edinburgh is true, I can't say," the cardinal archbishop of Westminster had stated to the same reporter who had interviewed the dubious dean. "All that the Catholic Church has to say on the matter has already been said. Miracles have occurred in the past and they are possible in the present as is indicated by the cures at Lourdes. But the Church has always hesitated to make the acceptance *de fide* of any particular miracle, except those upon which the essentials of the Christian religion are based, binding upon her children. And I think that you may take it from me that, even if the miracle which you mention has really occurred, Holy Church will allow the faithful to disbelieve in it as much as they want to." "*Ça se peut que ce soit un vrai miracle et ça se peut également que ce ne soit pas un vrai miracle*,"† had said the cardinal archbishop of Paris, and "*Se é vero é vero, ma, se non é vero, non é vero*,"‡ had said the cardinal archbishop of Milan, and "*Un milagro que es verdaderamente un milagro vale dos Milagros*,"§ had said the cardinal archbishop of Seville. And his lordship the bishop of Midlothian, on being asked by a representative of the Cowdenbeath *Sunday at Home* what he thought of recent events in his diocese, had blown his nose on a dirty pocket handkerchief and said: "Aye, aye, when the ca-a-at's away, the mice will play."

And today, Monday, the twelfth of December, the newspapers were swollen with badly digested miracle. Murders and abductions had been rare of late and, as it had been at least six weeks since a university don had been taken in amorous delight in Hyde Park and four months since a lady typist had flown the Atlantic, the miracle, as far as the journalists were concerned, had fallen as manna upon a sensationless world. It was, of course, difficult for them adequately to describe an event which their philosophy or lack of it declared to be impossible. But they had been too long accustomed to the job of supporting and abetting a Christianity which was tacitly assumed to be untrue not to be able to make a decent show without in any way committing their high impartiality. WONDER DANCE HALL STILL ON

† "It is possible that it is a true miracle, and it is equally possible that it is not a true miracle."

‡ "If it is true it is true, but if it is not true it is not true."

§ "A miracle which is a true miracle is worth two miracles."

BASS ROCK; FATHER MALACHY SAYS ACT OF GOD. IS ISAAC NEWTON DISCREDITED? DRAMATIC STORY OF SCOTTISH MYSTERY MONK'S LIFE ran some of the headlines. Yet, startling though they were intended to be, the headlines somehow failed to reflect the reality. Perhaps it was because it was difficult for political and other kinds of correspondents to write about the supernatural or perhaps it was because, having so often applied the word "wonder" to super-marmalade factories and the word "drama" to taxicab accidents and the word "mystery" to the disappearance of girls of eighteen, reporters found themselves at a loss for terms when confronted with an event which was really a wonder, a drama, and a mystery.

But, anyway, bald headlines or bad headlines, miracle or mass-hypnotism, it seemed that Father Malachy was well on his way to becoming as important as the Prince of Wales or Mr. Michael Arlen and that in a very short time his opinions on the merits of health salts and fountain pens would be treated, when expressed, as apocalyptic utterances. So that, all things considered, it was not to be wondered at that, after supernaturalizing his actions, he naturalized his thoughts on that Monday morning within the first octave of the translation of the Garden of Eden.

2.

BUT it was not for long that he was able to think over recent events and to wonder whether God would convince the whole world of their reality, for Canon Geoghegan, in his nobby cassock with the purple buttonholes, entered and said:

"I'm sorry to disturb you, Father, but Plus Bobbie's just arrived and he says that he would like to see you immediately."

"*Plus Bobbie?*" Father Malachy's voice was all interrogation.

"Our little nickname for his lordship," the canon explained. "It was, I think, Father Neary who invented it. You know the way bishops sign their names." He took a stub of pencil and printed on the margin of the front page of the *Scotsman*: ✠ ROBERT GILLESPIE. "Well, well, even the most loyal must have their little disloyalties, mustn't they? And when you have seen the right reverend gentleman I am sure that you will agree with me that the *sobriquet* is well found."

"I see." Father Malachy began to fold his napkin as methodically as though it were altar linen. "About the miracle, I suppose. And may I ask what attitude he seems to take up?"

"I am afraid, Father, that he is still inclined to regard it as unproven. He says—and not without reason, I think—that it has never been the policy of the Catholic Church to define any event, however supernatural in origin it may seem to be, as a miracle until all other philosophic and physical possibilities have been exhausted. He instances, naturally enough, the cures of organic diseases at Lourdes which everyone knows to be miracles and which the Church will not define as such from motives of holy prudence. He also says that some of the miracles which the more irresponsible of the saints have been pleased to work in Spain have retarded rather than advanced the Catholic cause. Of course, Father, I do not need to tell you that I personally am wholly convinced of the reality of the miracle. So, for that matter, are Fathers Neary and O'Flaherty; and indeed Father O'Flaherty was ill enough advised to tell his lordship that only a moth-eaten, atheistic Mormon could disbelieve in such a holy wonder of God. But, if you don't mind, I think that we had better go at once, as by nature he is impatient and does not like to be kept waiting."

They adjourned to the room in which Father Malachy and Canon Geoghegan had first made each other's acquaintance and where they found the bishop seated in the most important chair. His lips were pursed in a thoroughly Pictish manner and he was drumming his long fingers on the shiny knees of his trousers. He was a man of about fifty years of age and carried his six feet three inches so gracelessly that, even when sitting, he looked as though he must have a bad time of it when getting into railway carriages. About his colourless, unlighted eyes was the bleary expression of an unhappy cabman and his nose, red from the first Sunday in Advent to the last after Pentecost, seemed as though it must always be running. His long black coat, as uncomely as any country parson's, flowed from him drearily as though trying to symbolize an unmanicured temptation as seen by God; but between his collar and his waistcoat there peeped out a patch of purple to show that the Holy Spirit had been conferred upon him to such an extent that he himself was qualified to confer It upon others.

"Well, well," he said as Father Malachy went down on one knee before him and kissed the ring on his finger, "this is a pretty kettle of fish, isn't it?" And, indeed, as he uttered the words and peered into Father Malachy's face, he looked, with his ghoulish eyes and blubbery nose, not unlike a fishmonger examining a creel of newly caught haddocks. "A pretty kettle of fish," he repeated and stared gloomily across to the window where Fathers Neary and O'Flaherty, ordained boys of twenty-five years of age, were standing scratching unbrushed heads with red, mutton-chop hands.

"My lord, I agree with you." Father Malachy had ceased to bend over the episcopal bauble and was now holding himself upright and speaking with quiet determination. "It is a *very* pretty kettle of fish. Indeed, with your lordship's permission, I will go so far as to describe it as a glorious kettle of fish. For surely it is not every day that Almighty God condescends to work a miracle for the guidance and instruction of His people."

The bishop sat for a long time without saying anything. He wore on his face that absorbed expression of unabsorption which, when it was directed in tram cars upon his breviary, had earned for him from the unsuspecting the title of "yon saft meenister who's for aye readin' his Bibul in the trarm."

"Aye," he said at length. "But why did ye never let on?"

"Why did I never let on?" Father Malachy repeated the Caledonianism in a tone which showed clearly that he had but imperfectly understood it.

"Aye. Why didn't ye tell me about it? Surely if a buddy wants to go sticking his finger into miracles the bishop of the diocese has got a right to be in the know."

Father Malachy remembered the words with which Canon Geoghegan had assented to the proposed miracle: "All right. But not a word to the bishop, mind. He mightn't like it." He decided, however, that it would be hitting below the girdle to drag the canon into the affair and said:

"My lord, if I have displeased you I must humbly ask your pardon and forgiveness. And I must also ask you to believe that, in acting as I did, I did so for the honour and glory of our Lord and Saviour Jesus Christ and not to further any petty personal ambition. I believed—and I know now that I was—that I was acting under the guidance of the Holy Ghost and such scruples as I had about not making my intentions known to your lordship I silenced by telling myself that, though a priest is bound to obtain a faculty from the bishop of any diocese in which he proposes to hear confessions, canon law says nothing about such a faculty being necessary for a priest who intends to perform a miracle. Bernadette, I would respectfully remind your lordship, did not have to have a permit from the bishop of Tarbes before she could see Our Blessed Lady in the grotto at Lourdes."

"Aye," said the bishop grumpily, "that's as may be. But it seems to me that seeing Our Lady in the grotto at Lourdes and making a dance hall fly through the air are two very different cups of tea."

"My lord, both miracles were dependent upon the grace of God. Bernadette required the grace of God to see Our Lady just as much as Our Lady required the grace of God to appear to Bernadette. And I, my lord, required the grace of God to remove the Garden of Eden."

The bishop snuffled away inside his long, red nose.

"Your miracle strikes me as being too new-fangled," he said. "'*Nihil innovetur nisi quod traditum, est,*'[†] Father. And I don't think

† "Let there be no innovations except those which have been handed down."

that you can deny that making a dancing hall go gallivanting about the air has any precedent in tradition or holy legend."

"And what precedent, my lord, had tradition or holy legend when they were neither tradition nor holy legend but merely the outward and visible side of everyday Christianity?" Father Malachy, aware of the great danger of spiritual pride, took pains to keep all suggestion of disrespect from his voice. "For both tradition and holy legend have had a beginning." He smiled sadly as a thought came to him and he expressed it. "If your lordship will pardon the observation, I think that it is rather a pity that the laity should spend so much of their time in trying to make a legend out of present-day actualities and the clergy in trying to make present-day actualities out of legends. I am not, heaven be my witness, so foolish as to think that truth changes with the ages; but I do think that Almighty God, since He made time as well as eternity, is not averse from using the material objects peculiar to any particular time for the furtherance of His divine purposes. For when Our Blessed Lord changed water into wine at the wedding feast in Cana of Galilee He was being every bit as 'new-fangled' as He was when He permitted me to transfer the Garden of Eden to the Bass Rock. And I would remind you, my lord, that it was He Who gave me the power to perform this miracle. '*Non quod sufficientes simus cogitare aliquid a nobis, quasi ex nobis: sed sufficientia nostra ex Deo est,*'[†] as Saint Paul says. In other words and in another dialect, it wasna me."

"It wasna you, wasn't it?" The bishop nodded over the words as though they were a piece of writing which he could not decipher. "Aye, aye. And our sufficiency is from God, is it? Well, well. Perhaps you wouldn't mind going on with your story, Father—Father Malachy." He let his face slide into the palm of his hand, closed his eyes, and appeared to have gone to sleep. "It's all right," he said, seemingly to dispel the illusion. "Ah'm listening to ye."

† "Not that we are sufficient to think anything of ourselves; but our sufficiency is from God."

Father Malachy glanced quickly round the room. Canon Geoghegan was standing slightly behind him and wore the mask-like countenance of a cardinal assisting at a rather boring consistory. Fathers Neary and O'Flaherty, over by the window, had ceased to scratch their heads and were looking like a couple of flabbergasted schoolboys, and the Right Reverend Monsignor Robert Gillespie, Lord Bishop of Midlothian, having said that he was listening, had slouched further into a pose of inattention. The brown curtains, billowing slightly in a draught, seemed the most lively objects in the room and it was to them that, after bowing in the direction of the huddled bishop, he made his *apologia.*

"My lord bishop," he said to the curtains as in and out they flapped, "it is manifest to the least observant of us that this is a very godless age. Indeed, so godless is it that the godlessness of former ages appears almost pious by contrast. For the godlessness of former ages consisted more in forgetting God than in denying Him, whereas the godlessness of today is a real revolt against God as God and heaps ridicule upon those who would remember Him. The truths of our holy religion: the Blessed Sacrament, the prestige in heaven of the Mother of God, the divinity of Our Blessed Lord are regarded and publicly described as anthropomorphic misconceptions by high philosophers and scientists. In Britain we who have the Faith are but a handful as compared with those who rejoice that they are not encumbered with any such mediaeval superstition. In France the Catholic religion has been trampled on by the lusts of the flesh disguised as pride of intellect, and in Italy and South America the religion which satisfied Augustine and Aquinas is coming to be looked upon as mainly a woman's affair. And even in the only two sane countries left in the world, even in Spain and Ireland, even in Compostella and by Killarney are the grand facts of Catholicism becoming swamped under Paris hats and New York economics. The Catholic religion, my lord, is not only beautiful; it is also true. The Blessed Sacrament is not only a poetic conception of the Divine

Presence; it is also a harder and more permanent reality than Throgmorton Street on a wet afternoon. Our Blessed Lord is not merely a pale figure moving through the Gospels in lovely Latin; He is also Very God of Very God and will judge those who don't believe in Him just as impartially as He will those who do. And modernist sinners who die in the state of final impenitence will not be able to escape hell on the grounds that no educated reader of the *Daily Mail* believes in it.

"My lord, Our Blessed Lord came down from heaven to die for our sins and to form a church which should apply the benefits of His atonement to the souls of men and women. That church we know to be the Catholic Church because it is the only church which reaches back to the descent of the Holy Ghost upon the Apostles and because it alone bears the marks of uniformity in time and in space by which men may know the Bride of Christ. '*Euntes, ergo, docete omnes gentes,*'† Our Blessed Lord commanded the Apostles before He ascended into heaven, and to Greece and to Russia and to Scotland and to Iceland they and their successors went, teaching all men and baptizing them in the Name of the Father and of the Son and of the Holy Ghost, casting out devils and healing the sick and bringing the white peace of Christ in the folds of their robes. The result of their teaching was the Ages of Faith in which, if there was disobedience to God, there was at least the conviction that the things of heaven were permanent and that the things of earth were transitory. Then came the Reformation and the great attack upon Christian doctrine, of which the results can be clearly seen today. From rejecting the Mass men have passed to rejecting Him Who founded the Mass and from rejecting Him Who founded the Mass they have passed to that dreadful apathy in spirituals which is the cause of all the most repugnant characteristics of contemporary civilization. And yet, my lord, the Catholic religion is just as true today as it was when Columba first set sail for Iona." He

† "Go ye, therefore, and teach all nations."

smiled as he noticed that the curtains were still now and he perorated to them in gratitude for their attention: "Behind trams and talking pictures and Wall Street the realities of God go on like the wheels behind the face of a watch which men are too unskilled to open. There is heaven and there is hell and there is purgatory, and Mary prays for sinners and the Holy Ghost goes coasting about the world like a wise old wind. Francis Thompson was a realist as well as a poet when he wrote:

'The angels keep their ancient places—
Turn but a stone and start a wing!
'Tis ye, 'tis your estrangèd faces,
That miss the many-splendoured thing.

'But (when so sad thou can'st not sadder)
Cry; and upon thy so sore loss
Shall shine the traffic of Jacob's ladder
Pitched between Heaven and Charing Cross.'"

"'Turrn but a stone and starrt a wing,'" the bishop interrupted to requote. "Aye, aye, and so instead of turning a stone ye flitted a dancing hall? Is that what ye mean?"

"Precisely," Father Malachy was going to say when the door opened and James, the house factotum, entered and announced to Canon Geoghegan:

"Yer riverince, there's a man downstairs with a nice fresh complexion like yourself and he's afther seein' Father Malachy here about the miracle. He says his name is Gillespie and, now that I come to think of it, he's not unlike his lordship the bishop there. And, saving your riverind prisinces, he's got a fancy piece of goods with him. You know. The kind his lordship's always writing pastorals about."

3.

"JAMES," said the canon, breaking in upon the silence which followed this descent of the ridiculous upon the sublime, "how often have I told you that it is not your place to comment upon the characteristics of visitors to the clergy house. And his lordship the bishop must, I am sure, find your impertinent references to himself in very bad taste."

But James was not at all discomfited.

"Sure," he said, "and there was no harm intinded at all. And sure if I hadn't been afther tellin' ye that the colleen looked more loik Mary Pickford than Blessed Mother Margaret Alacoque it's yer riverince who'd be afther pullin' me ears."

The canon took no notice of James's defense but addressed himself to the bishop.

"My lord," he said, "if what the boy says is true it would seem that it is your lordship's brother who wants to see Father Malachy. Perhaps, under the circumstances..."

The bishop suddenly sat up, blinked his eyes, and began to take a more evident interest in what was happening around him.

"Aye," he said. "It'll be Aundry as like as not. Mebbe he's been at some of his carryings-on. Mebbe even he was in that paly de donce when it was flitted. He was always a great boy for the dancing, was Aundry. Ah remember as a bairn he used to be awfy fond of Hulla-ballu-ballu Hulla-ballu-balli and Jingaring. Perhaps, though, if there'd been more Shall We Gather at the River and less Hulla-ballu-ballu Aundry wouldn't have been such a bard lard as he is today. But if Father Malachy here has no objection to seeing him, then Ah see no reason why the interview should not take place in ma presence. And Ah'd like fine to have a peek at the lassie that Aundry's traipsing round with. For upon ma wurrd, Canon, what with lassies and all yon dancin' it's pretty difficult for a non-churrch-going Presbyterian like Aundry to keep his bapteesmal innocence. Aye, aye, we'd better have a look at the two of them."

The canon turned to James.

"Show them both up here," he said sharply.

Father Malachy wondered for a moment as to whether he should go on with his *apologia,* but he judged, from the expression on the bishop's face and from those on the faces of the other three priests, that he was not expected to do so. Canon Geoghegan, however, seized the opportunity of offering his excuses for James's familiar mode of address.

"I must apologize, my lord, for that boy," he said. "But I simply can't get him to speak respectfully to or of his superiors. Only last week Mrs. Gore-Whisket—one of our most important converts—called to see me and James announced her to me as 'an old hag whose face doesn't match the rest of her body'; by which he meant that Mrs. Gore-Whisket, who is a vain and frivolous woman, disobeys what I may call the toilet rubrics of His Holiness Pope Pius the Eleventh and paints her face as though she were a light woman in Budapesth or the Book of Proverbs. But, of course, she is nothing of the sort, my lord; she lives in Murrayfield and is a regular attendant at all the meetings of the *Bona Mors* Society. And, as for James, it is in speech rather than in deed that he errs for he serves my Mass each morning at eight and goes to Holy Communion every day of his life."

The bishop nodded heavily.

"The laddie strikes me as being all right," he said. "And so he goes to Holy Communion every day, does he? Well now, fancy that. And, mind you, Ah'd far rather have a laddie with a bee in his bonnet and God in his soul than one of those clever ones who are all genuflections and no rosary. Aye, and that's the sober truth that Ah'm telling ye. Aye." The bishop's chin sank back onto the patch of purple beneath his collar. "Aye," he sighed rather than said and closed his eyes and was silent.

But it was not for long that his chin remained there for, almost as soon as the last sentence had passed from his mouth to the minds of his hearers, the door opened again and the Bee Bee Bee and Bubbles were brushed into the room by an expressive wave of James's hand.

Bubbles came first, with those short, mincing steps with which Agag is recorded to have approached Samuel and with which *mannequins* in the Rue de la Paix work such harm to the souls of the weak in spirit and strong in flesh. She was wearing a pale green coat which she held tightly about her as though it were the only garment which she had on. But beneath it there peeped out, as pale and as green, the margin of a frock, fluted and silken, which wooed her legs and made tempting little sounds as she walked. Her hat was black, a close-fitting crown with a silver brooch in it, and her shoes were high-heeled and shiny. Flip, flip, flip she came, like a courtesan coming to Anthony in the desert, and the bishop and Canon Geoghegan and Father Malachy and Father Neary and Father O'Flaherty, for all that they had been consecrated to God, looked so hardly at her that they almost failed to notice her cavalier who, blue-suited and bespatted, followed dully in her train like a piece of unremarkable prose coming after an exquisite line of poetry.

It was, however, the cavalier and not the cavaliered who spoke. Bubbles didn't know the bishop or any of the other four clergymen who were standing, their black clothes dripping from them like graceless ink, awkwardly about the room and so, at a distance of about three yards; from Christ's representative in Midlothian, she stopped and allowed the Bee Bee Bee to precede her and, as she silently phrased it in the secret parts of her consciousness, to do all the pow-wowing.

"Well, Bobbie, just fancy meeting you here," the Bee Bee Bee greeted. "Ah'd heard from a felly in F. and F.'s that you were over in Cowdenbeath holding a consummation, whatever that may mean."

The bishop, whose chin was now well away from the purple and whose eyes were more for Bubbles than for his brother, said testily:

"Confirmation, Aundry, confirmation. And it means imparting the Holy Spurrit to folk to give them strength to keep the promises which were made for them at their bapteesm. And by the same token, Aundry, a good dose of the same medicine wouldn't do ye any harm." His eyes became all for Bubbles. "And who's the lassie, Aundry?

Who's the lassie?"

"She's ma wee hen," said the Bee Bee Bee, blushing.

"Your wee hen?"

"Aye. Ma ain wee snooky. Ma wee Scotch haggis. Ah call her Bubbles, but her right name's Peggy McNab and soon it's going to be Peggy Gillespie—Mistress Peggy Gillespie. She used to teach dancing over by." He jerked his head towards where the Garden of Eden used to be, and then, addressing Peggy, continued: "Bubbles, this is ma big, releegious brother. He's a popey bishop and burns candles all the year round but he's not a bad sort when ye get to know him. That's right. Shake hands with him. He looks a big Ally Sloper but he can be as nice as sausages when he likes."

The bishop half rose from his chair and, bending his head and smiling his most secular smile, shook hands with Bubbles who half-curtsied and said: "Pleased to meet you, mister." Then, whisking his coattails from where they had whisked themselves, he sat down again and became once more the *sacerdos magnus,* who was more accustomed to have authority than to be under it.

"Aye," he said, "and so ye was thinking of getting married, Aundry, was ye?"

"Ah was that," said the Bee Bee Bee.

"Fancy that now," said the bishop.

"Aye, just fancy," said the Bee Bee Bee.

"Aye," said the bishop, "just fancy."

"Yes," said the Bee Bee Bee, "just fancy."

The bishop again concentrated his gaze upon Bubbles, whose pale green clothes seemed to fill the room with their colour. A wee bit worldly, he decided, and not over-given to thoughts about the hereafter. But then Aundry himself was such a harum-scarum that no really devout woman, Catholic or Protestant, would look twice at him. Taught dancing, too? Och, well, people talked an awful lot about dancing, but at least half of it was sheer haver and it was as like as not that she taught the half which, if it wasn't apostolic, was not necessarily diabolic. Aye, aye, aye. There was dancing and dancing and the lassie, for all her powder and paint and faldarals, seemed a nice enough wee bairn. Och, well, and Aundry, with all his whiskers and daundering about, was not the sort of man to marry the serious go-to-meeting sort of woman. Och, well. Aye, aye, aye.

"Sit ye down," he said as genially as he could, "sit ye down."

They sat down: Bubbles carefully, keeping the custody of her frock and crossing her legs in such a manner that her knees should not be seen; the Bee Bee Bee jauntily, as though he owned the chair and didn't give a damn for anybody. And the four priests, who had been standing since the beginning of the interview, interpreted the episcopal invitation as including them and sat down on the nearest chairs which they could find.

"Aye," said the bishop to his brother, "and so ye was wanting to see Father Malachy here, was ye?"

The Bee Bee Bee nodded.

"Ah was that. Ye see, it's like this. Bubbles and I were in the Garden of Eden when it fleed away. Now, if that doesn't set me thinking on the old song, Bobbie. Ye know it, don't ye? About three craws sittin' on a wa' and the first and second craw fleeing roond the wa' and the third craw not being able to flee at a'. Well, all that Ah can say is that this particular craw fleed and fleed and fleed—just like Eyetalian sliders in the summer. The Garden of Eden, I mean."

"Aye," said the bishop, "it seems to have fleed all right."

"Aye, it did that." The Bee Bee Bee glanced first at the bishop and then at the four priests and finally at Bubbles, who, all silken and green, looked like a slender fern growing on a heap of slag. "Ah had just popped the question to Peg here and she had said that she would be very pleased to be Mistress Gillespie and that she'd like fine to go for a little ta-ta by the briny and Ah had told the laddie at the door to look slippy about getting a taxi. Well, to cut a long story short, Ah had sent for a taxi and was waiting and waiting with Peg here who looked just like a wee stotty ball in her coat and hat. And while we were waiting and waiting Ah told her how nice it would be to go for a hurl in a taxi and she told me—och, well, never mind what she told me but it was awfy passionate and would have looked fine on the fillums. Ye know the sort of thing: 'Ma heart beats for you like a drum sounding across the waves of eturrnity' and all yon. Well, as Ah was saying, we were waiting and waiting and waiting and all thae theatrical lassies were gallivanting about like a lot of bumble-bees having a mighty good bumble to themselves. A pretty lot of lassies they were, all slim and slithery, ye know, like bad women from Paris leading Elders o' the Kirk into temptation. Well, as Ah was saying, we were waiting and waiting and talking away like two commercial travellers in Hawick and never a sign of the taxi or of the laddie who had gone to fetch it and all thae theatrical lassies were moving about and dancing and carrying on with the laddies. Well, after about half an hour of standing and standing, Ah thought that something queer must have happened to the laddie so Ah told Peg here to wait for me and went out to see what was up. Mind ye, Ah thought that the air was a bit fresh when Ah got outside and Ah mind wondering why Ah couldna see the lights on the other side of the street. However, Ah didn't bother ma head about that and Ah went down the steps like a lamplighter and slipped on a bit of slimy rock and nearly went head over heels into the sea."

"Ye what?" The bishop was all goggling eyes and open mouth. "Ye what? Say that again, Aundry."

"Ah slipped on a bit of slimy rock and nearly went head over heeds into the sea," the Bee Bee Bee repeated. "But Ah managed to clamber back all right and then Ah found that Ah was on the Bass Rock. Aye, Bobbie, smile if ye will. But it wasna a Sunday school outing, All can tell ye."

"Ah'm no smiling, Aundry." The bishop, in his emotion, became doubly Scots. "But are ye sure that ye're no makin' a mistake? Are ye sure that ye hadna taken a boat out to the Bass Rock like and dreamt ye were dancing and all that?"

"You're a fine one, Bobbie, and no mistake." The Bee Bee Bee shook his head in deliberate pity. "Ah couldna dream that Ah was awake, could I? And that the Garden of Eden was sticking on the Bass Rock like as though it had been built there. Ah couldna dream that the basement fitted into the rock like a knife into a bit of plum duff and that the lassies were all as feared as feared could be. Ah might have dreamt it but if Ah did, Ah'm dreaming now and you're still in Cowdenbeath fiddling away at your silly consummation. Aye, and Bubbles must have dreamt it, too, and the theatrical lassies and the manager, who's a great big feardie if ever there was one. Aye, and Ah must have dreamt about us all sleeping on tables and chairs and things and Ah must have dreamt about the lighthouse-keeper climbing up to find out what had happened and about the lifeboat rescuing us and about us getting our photies taken for the *Daily Mail* and about ma coming here to see Father Malachy. Aye, Bobbie, Ah must have been doing an awfy lot of dreaming."

The bishop nodded his head gravely.

"That's so," he said. "But did ye no feel the fleeing when the fleeing was on?"

"No," said the Bee Bee Bee humourlessly, "there was no sea-sickness about the business at all." He was silent for a moment and appeared to be thinking inwards rather than outwards. "Aye," he went on, "and, what with the wind blowing about like the wrath of God and Bubbles here weeping like a two-year-old and thae chorus lassies yelling and shrieking like a lot of dying pigs, we had a mighty fine time, Ah can tell ye. And us not knowing whether the end of the wurrld had come and no decent beds to sleep upon forby. Ah wasna sorry when the morning came and we got taken ashore. And then Ah read in the papers that this priestie here"—he jerked his head in the direction of Father Malachy—"had done all yon fiddle-sticks to prove the power o' God or some such blether."

"Aye, aye," said the bishop as his mind pondered the eternal verities and their reflection through the ages, "the power o' God is a wonderful thing."

"So," concluded the Bee Bee Bee, glancing at Bubbles as though to include her judgment with his, "Ah just called in to tell Father Malachy here that Ah didn't believe a word of all yon humbuggery and nonsense."

4.

THEY went as they had come: Bubbles with her coat wrapped tightly about her like Cleopatra passing through her eunuchs on the way to her bath, the Bee Bee Bee insignificantly, like a domesticated Mark Anthony without any battles to lose.

"Aye," said the bishop when the door had closed behind them, "that just lets ye shows ye. Aundry wouldn't believe in hell fire even if he were kept there for a month of eternities."

"In that," said Father Malachy, "he is not unlike some of our more famous spiritual leaders whose ecclesiastical preferment is due to the fact that they disbelieve in more than their colleagues. Indeed, we all know of one prelate who expresses in the language of Isaiah the theology of bank clerks and who, when he is conducted to the gates of hell, will protest that the place doesn't exist and that he has several times described it as an exploded superstition in the pages of the *Evening Flag*. Your brother, my lord, who has been—if one may say so—in the thick of the miracle and doesn't believe in it is only another instance of the dogmatism of a race which says that there is no such thing as dogma. For the modernists, from those who read philosophy to those who play the gramophone, assert that all dogmas are untrue, save the dogma that there is no dogma."

"Aye," said the bishop, "it strikes me that yon miracle of yours is going to be a bit of a botheration."

"My lord," Canon Geoghegan interposed, "I think, if you will permit me to say so, that you are wrong. Since the miracle took place I have been requested by three ladies of the High Anglican inaccuracy to instruct them in the doctrines of the Catholic Church; and I feel sure that, as the authenticity of the miracle becomes more widely known, these applications will be followed by others. After all, your brother is a notoriously unspiritual person and it is not altogether to be wondered at that he should be unwilling to believe in what is, for him, a shattering of his most cherished materialisms. I must admit, however, that as yet neither the professor of physics at the university nor the lord provost of Edinburgh has presented himself for catechetical instruction, but I see no reason why, within the next few days, we should not be enriched by many important conversions."

"Mebbe aye and mebbe no and mebbe Inverary," said the bishop. "In other wurrds, Ah'm no so sure. Miracles were all very well in the days when saints were treated like Harry Lauder; but in these days of whisky and disbelief and what not... Ye all heard what Aundry said? He was in yon paly de donce when it deed away and he says that he doesn't believe in the miracle. Now what can ye make of a daftie like yon?"

Father Malachy spoke again, gently, persuasively.

"In any case," he said, "I hope that your lordship has no longer any doubts as to the reality of the wonder which was worked on Saturday night by the grace of God. And, if there rest any misgivings in your mind as to the purity of my motives, surely the fact that God *did* make the Garden of Eden fly through the air is sufficient testimony that I was not seeking personal notoriety. For, even although the doctrine has never been defined by any council of theologians, it is evident that Almighty God does not override the natural laws in order that an insignificant Benedictine monk may get his name into the papers. And, again, even if only one soul is brought to the truth by this translation of the Garden of Eden, then the miracle has not been in vain. For Our Blessed Lord loves all souls with an equal and limitless love and the salvation of the shoeless prostitute is as dear to His Sacred Heart as that of His vicar in Rome. There are hierarchies of order, my lord, but there are no hierarchies of title to grace. And it was to bring in the lame, the halt, and the blind, the biologist, the engineer, and the light-o'-love that I begged Our Lord to grant me the power to perform this miracle."

The bishop had been nodding his head all the time that Father Malachy had been speaking.

"Aye," he said, "Ah'm beginning to think that your miracle is the real Mackay, all right. Aundry's not the sort of person to imagine that a building's been fleeing when it's been standing still. But what bothers me is what the Pope's going to say about it. And all thae scarlet runners that he's got about him. They are not the sort of folks that swallow miracles easily. They'll appoint commissions to inquire into the matter and mebbe in about a hundred years' time the miracle will be declared to be genuine. Till then Ah suppose the Garden of Eden will go on sitting on the Bass Rock and the faithful will be free to believe that it's still here in Edinburgh or in Copenhagen. The mills of God grind slowly, Father, and miracles require a mighty lot of minting before they can have '*nihil obstat*' stamped on them."

"But surely," Father Malachy protested, "it will be obvious to any unprejudiced person that the Garden of Eden couldn't have got onto the Bass Rock by any natural means."

Once again Canon Geoghegan interrupted in his high monotone.

"My dear Father," he said, "I am afraid that there are very few unprejudiced persons in the world. People generally try to make facts fit philosophies rather than to make philosophies fit facts. As an instance of this I have only to tell you that, while you were having breakfast this morning, Mr. Humphrey Hamilton called to tell me that, as he had taken the science tripos at Cambridge, he was convinced that the translation of the Garden of Eden was no translation at all but an illusion, like that of the fakir throwing a rope into the air and climbing up it and disappearing, produced by mass-hypnotism."

"Ah wouldn't pay much attention to a scallywag like him," said the bishop. "Only last Wednesday Ah saw him on top of a tram reading a novel by Elinor Glyn. Sure as death that's the truth Ah'm telling ye."

Canon Geoghegan and Father Neary and Father O'Flaherty, to whom any novel in which men and women made love competently was *anathema maranatha*, looked very grave and each of them made a silent resolution to preach at the earliest opportunity on the folly of reading any book in which the characters did not all become Catholics on the last page.

"Aye," the bishop re-mumbled, "a scallywag. And he wears grey flannels and a yelly straw hat in the summer time. Many's the time Ah've seen him swa-anking along Princes Street like Saint Augustine before he saw the light. Aye, and with strippit socks on, too."

Father Malachy, perceiving that the conversation was switching from the miraculous to the material, said:

"My lord, I quite realize the point which you have just made and I know that Rome is slow to move because she does not wish, through hastiness or lack of reflection, to prejudice the cause of Christ throughout the world. But here in the diocese of Midlothian we have seen with our own eyes and heard with our own ears and we know that God has wrought a great miracle for the conversion of the heathen in our midst and for the encouragement of those who, possessing and professing the Faith, find it difficult, in workshop or in office, to correspond with the grace which comes to them from above. I think, therefore, that it behoves us to use this opportunity of quickening the spiritual life of those souls which have been committed to your lordship's charge."

"Aye," said the bishop, "Ah'm all in favour of that. Some of ma bonny bairns in God want a good talking to, there's no denying that. A little less picture house and a little more Benediction wouldn't do a lot of folk any harm."

"My lord," Canon Geoghegan began in his parsonical wail, "I think that you must admit that it is most significant that Almighty God should have chosen to remove from the parish an establishment which, if it wasn't Continental, was peninsular rather than insular in its customs. The Garden of Eden has always been the cause of a great deal of sensuality in my parish, and I, for one, am heartily thankful for its removal."

"Sensuality?" The bishop was again speaking to his purple patch. "You mean boys and girls carrying on, don't ye?"

"I do," said Canon Geoghegan. "And carrying on and carrying on and carrying on."

"Dearie me," said the bishop, "that's a turrible state of affairs."

"Faith," said Father Neary, "and it's from my own bedroom window that I've been after seeing things that were worse than I've read about in moral theology."

The bishop was just going to say what he thought—that the teaching of the French language ought to be forbidden in Catholic schools—when there came from outside a burst of music and the sound of voices singing raggedly "Hail, Queen of Heaven, the Ocean Star." Moved simultaneously by the same impulse, the bishop and the four priests rose from their chairs and went quickly to the window where, pulling back the curtains, they saw that a surpliced procession had halted in front of the former site of the Garden of Eden and that a clergyman wearing a white cope was censing the place where the main entrance had been. The crowd was so great that there were at least ten policemen occupied in controlling its surgings and four cinematographers were gaily turning handles.

"If it isn't that arch-pretender Meaty," Canon Geoghegan said angrily. "Not content with stealing our hymns, our vestments, and our liturgy, he is now doing his best to pocket our miracle."

"Meaty?" The bishop was puzzled, and looked it. "Meaty? Who's Meaty?"

"He's the rector of the Anglican church at St. Gabriel," the canon explained. "He calls himself 'Father' and spits in his sanctuary as, having once been on a Cook's tour to Rome, he imagines that the habit has the authority of the Sacred Congregation of Rites."

"The ould thief," said Father Neary.

"Sure and he has no right at all to pinch our darlin' miracle," said

Father O'Flaherty.

The bishop, pressing his nose against the window-pane and breathing a hectagon of mist over it, came quickly to a decision.

"Aye," he said, "the miracle's a wurrk of God all right. And Aundry couldn't have been mistaken about all yon fleeing any more than I can be mistaken about yon paly de donce being no longer there. Besides, we canna have the Piskies lifting our miracle like this. It'll be the Presbies next and then the Congregationalists and all thae dreich heretics. So let it be clearly understood, Canon, that I, Robert, Bishop of Midlothian, order, by the authority given to me from God through our Holy Father the Pope, that a solemn procession to the scene of the miracle take place every afternoon this week and that the *Te Deum* be pontifically chanted by myself; and ye might as well see to it that there are some of thae cinema fellies on the spot and if ye show me where your telephone is Ah'll say how-d'ye-do to the parish priest of North Berwick and tell him to go out in a boat and sprinkle a wee bit holy water over the Bass Rock."

CHAPTER VII

1.

About the same time as the lord bishop of Midlothian was interviewing Father Malachy the station at North Berwick was gay with slim young legs and bright frocks. For the chorus ladies of the *Whose Baby Are You?* company, after having been entertained at breakfast by the management of the Marine Hotel, were all fluttering about the platform in very worldly clothes and, with their golden hair and ebony hair and with their high heels and with their lips like rivers of blood, were looking just as though they had been in no miracle at all. Swish, swish, swish they went, in crimsons, in greens and in blues, shrilling here, trilling there as, with *Happy Magazines* and *Passing Shows* and boxes of chocolates under their arms, they climbed into third-class compartments and were absorbed by them, like different coloured inks being sucked into dirty bottles.

And behind them, or rather not quite behind them—for he was going as fast as his fat little legs would carry him—came Mr. George Bleater, their manager. He was a broad man with a large bullet head and stupid brown eyes and a face that had long been dyed a deep damask by excessive bibbing. He was fifty-nine years of age, was Mr.

George Bleater, and was grey at the temples and bald underneath the bowler which he wore like a dismal crown more symbolic of servitude than of sovereignty. And this morning, as he shepherded his girls before him, he was in a roaring bad temper because they were due to open that night at Newcastle at seven o'clock and they ought to have arrived the previous day at noon.

Mr. George Bleater was a very dour Scot and he did not like having to spend money. Indeed, so little did he like to spend money that he grudged spending it on the commodity which gave him greatest enjoyment and so he managed, by insinuating himself into and withdrawing himself from groups in bars at the right moment, to get as much of it as he could for nothing. And yesterday and this morning he had been having to spend a very great deal of money on that which gave him no pleasure at all.

To begin with they had been rescued from the Bass Rock too late on Sunday morning for them to motor into Edinburgh to catch the one day train to Newcastle which a Scots god allowed the London & North Eastern Railway Company to run on the Sabbath; and in any case the girls, in spite of the fact that they had been sucking tangerine oranges and drinking lemonade all night, had been clamouring for breakfast. And by the time that they had finished that, at least half of them declared that they were too overcome with nervous exhaustion to be able to travel that day and at least another quarter had pointed out to him that they had reserved no lodgings in Newcastle and that, as the night train would not get them there until after one o'clock in the morning, they would have to stay the night in a hotel at his expense. And, as he had already booked the railway tickets from Edinburgh, he did not see that there was any economy to be made by hiring an omnibus or cars and making the journey by road. So he had just had to put his hand in his pocket and pay them all a day's meals and a night's rest at the Marine Hotel. Fortunately, however, the management had, by way of discount on so large a bill and in recognition of the fame which they had reflected on the hotel, presented them with their Monday morning's breakfast free gratis and for nothing.

His bad temper was calmed to a certain extent when, on entering a first-class smoking compartment, he found that it was already tenanted by Mr. J. Shyman Bell, manager and owner of the Garden of Eden.

Mr. J. Shyman Bell was about forty years of age and was even fatter than Mr. George Bleater and liked alcohol so much that he was willing, at all times and in all places, to pay for it. But whereas Mr. George Bleater's fatness was, to a certain extent, the earned stoutness of maturity, Mr. J. Shyman Bell's fatness was that premature and unhealthy flabbiness due to excess in drink and venery. His face, from which two small blue eyes peered numbly at the world, was a bright, brick red and, hanging down over his neck like a roll of incontinent blubber, resembled nothing so much as a grotesque red moon such as is sometimes painted on musical comedy scenery. And across this red moon there ran, like a furrow to make it look real, a scar which had been acquired in a fight at school which Mr. J. Shyman Bell had not quite succeeded in avoiding (during the war he had served his King and Country in Madrid). This scar he always tried to hide, when speaking or laughing, by an acquired mannerism of scratching the part between his left nostril and his left upper lip.

"Good morning, Mr. George Bleater," he greeted, looking up from the very popular daily newspaper which he had been scanning. (It was another of his mannerisms always to address people whom he didn't know very well by their Christian names as well as their surnames.) "Good morning, Mr. George Bleater. The papers are full of this most extraordinary happening, I see. Extraordinary, what?" And his thumb and forefinger went a-scratching interrogatively across the scar on his face.

Mr. George Bleater did not immediately reply. To tell the truth, he thought that Mr. J. Shyman Bell, although he drank whisky well enough to confirm his nationality, talked a little bit too much and too fluently to be a good Scot. So he sat down slowly, pulled up his neat blue trousers and, showing two margins of grey woollen sock surmounting his neat black boots, blinked and looked, as he really was, like a mass of anatomy whose sense perceptions were physical rather than mental.

"Pack of fiddle-faddle," he said. "Pack of English Church fiddle-faddle. Who's the Holy Ghost, anyway? Eh, tell me that. Who's the Holy Ghost, anyway? Well, I'll tell you if you can't tell me. The Holy Ghost's just a—just an imaginary imagination. In other words, just a piece of English Church fiddle-faddle."

"There's a prominent clergyman says here that the miracle is a scandal to Christendom and an insult to the modern mind," said Mr. J. Shyman Bell, rolling the quoted words lusciously round his tongue and booming them out as though it were a thousand Mr. George Bleaters that he was addressing. "And," he went on, reading now rather than quoting, "'such so-called manifestations of the supernatural are crude blasphemies against the spirit of an age which has learned to recite the Apostles' Creed with the same detached spirit as, during the late war, our soldiers sang "Colonel Bogey." If the Roman authorities hope to advance their cause in England by such obsolete wizardry, then I can only tell them that they are mistaken. To the educated mind the transference of an Edinburgh dancing hall to the top of the Bass Rock is no more a proof of the infallibility of the Pope than the production of a rabbit out of a conjuror's hat is a proof of the infallibility of the conjuror. In other words, all phenomena, no matter how extraordinary they may seem to be, are expressible in terms of natural laws; and some other answer than that given by sanctified hocus-pocus will have to be found for the event stated to have taken place on Saturday night.'" Mr. J. Shyman Bell's voice sank to a lower tone as, folding up his newspaper and tossing it a good yard along the blue-cushioned seat, he asked once more: "Extraordinary, what?"

Once again Mr. George Bleater did not immediately reply. The words had rung even more meaninglessly in his mind than they had been rung on Mr. J. Shyman Bell's lips (for Mr. Bell liked articulating words which sounded to him sonorous and did not particularly bother his head as to their meaning). But at last, rolling his brown eyes in pathetic inquiry, he said:

"I think that the Church has no business to interfere with people. The Holy Ghost indeed! And who is the Holy Ghost, I should like to know? Mind you, it's not the first time I've asked the question. Damn it, man, I've asked ministers and they haven't been able to tell me. So what I say is that the Holy Ghost is an imaginary imagination. Did you ever know anyone who'd seen a photograph of the Holy Ghost? I ask you, did you ever know anyone who'd seen a photograph of the Holy Ghost?"

Mr. J. Shyman Bell certainly did not remember having heard of anyone who had seen a photograph of the Holy Ghost. Indeed, never having taken a great interest in spiritual matters, he was almost as hazy as his questioner as to the identity and functions of the Person under discussion.

"Trinity," he said at length. "Trinity. That's it, Mr. George Bleater. The Holy Ghost's got something to do with the Trinity."

"Trinity." Mr. George Bleater repeated the familiar syllables and tried to accustom himself to their unfamiliar meaning; for, having toured theatrical companies in and around Edinburgh for nearly thirty years and having neglected to pay a visit to any place of worship for nearly forty, it was but natural that the word should connote for him the residential district in Leith called by that name rather than the theological conception which had caused the district to be so called. "Trinity. Oh, I see. You mean more of that English Church fiddle-faddle, don't you?"

Mr. J. Shyman Bell nodded.

"That's it, Mr. George Bleater. I see that you understand perfectly. God and the Virgin Mary and the Holy Ghost and all that." He paused, scratched his scar, and continued: "I must say that that's quite a nice set of birds that you've got in your company, what? Nice legs and figures that go in and come out at the proper places." He scratched his scar vigorously. "Not too virtuous, I suppose."

Now Mr. George Bleater was, in his vices, such a monotheist that, consecrating all his devotion to Bacchus, he had none left over for Venus. So Mr. J. Shyman Bell's compliments upon the hips and knees of the ladies of his chorus struck him as falling in the same category as remarks about rain or sunshine or the lack of either and as requiring no definite reply. ("Dear George," his not unintelligent wife used to remark to her friends, "is a most reliable sort of husband to have in the theatrical business although I must admit that what he doesn't give to the bust he takes out of the bottle.") Besides he was really puzzled as to how the Garden of Eden had come, from sitting in a street in Edinburgh, to place itself upon the Bass Rock. "I did so by the Holy Ghost within me," Father Malachy had been reported as saying by the North Berwick *Gull* and, having for a long time been trying, from motives of inquisitiveness rather than from those of erudition, to find out who the Holy Ghost was, he was as genuinely intrigued as the tissues of his fifth-rate cerebellum allowed him to be. And so, as the train slid out from the multi-coloured Oxo and Gold Flake and Edgar Wallace advertisements into the drab brown of the winter fields, he began again:

"Yes," he said, "that's all very well. But *who* is the Holy Ghost? That's what I want to know. A person or a thing or what? And why is it that nobody seems to be able to tell me who the Holy Ghost really is or was? Damn it, man, I've asked ministers and they haven't been able to tell me. Now, if I could see a picture or a photograph or a drawing or something. But do you think that anyone can show me one? Ministers even. I've asked ministers and they haven't been able to tell me. So what I say is that the Holy Ghost is an imaginary imagination just as—just as God is an imaginary imagination." And, having thus annihilated revelation from Alpha to Omega, he blinked polemically through his glasses at Mr. J. Shyman Bell as though challenging him to defend, if he could, the Christian Faith as delivered to and by the Apostles.

But Mr. J. Shyman Bell was as uninterested in the Holy Ghost as he was in the fauna and flora of Norway. He did not pretend to know how the Garden of Eden had got on the top of the Bass Rock, but he hoped, inarticulately, like all good businessmen the world over, that God had had nothing to do with it and, being an optimist like all good businessmen must be, he construed, like them, his inarticulate hope into the articulate conviction that miracles and all that were fakes and shams and frauds.

"Extraordinary, what? But I wouldn't bother my head about that if I were you, Mr. George Bleater. This clergyman here"—he reached out to tap the newspaper which he had flung aside—"says that it's all nonsense. And what's good enough for a famous dean like him ought to be good enough for you and me, Mr. George Bleater. Yes, all nonsense. These Catholics!" He made a gesture the expressiveness of which was mitigated by the podginess of his hands. "After all, we're men of the world, Mr. George Bleater, and we're not going to make fools of ourselves over Holy Ghosts and Holy This-es and Holy Thats. And if you'd lived abroad as much as I have, Mr. George Bleater, you'd know that the Catholic Church is all fairy tales and humbug. Why, in France the priests ride women's bicycles because of the long black skirts that they wear. Extraordinary, what? Now what I've always said is this: that a religion must be a pretty common sort of affair if its priests have got to ride women's bikes. Although, Mr. George Bleater, that is not to say that I wouldn't like to see some of your well-built young ladies doing the same thing, ha, ha."

Mr. George Bleater thought and thought and thought. Or, rather, Mr. George Bleater did not think and did not think and did not think. For so whiskied was his brain that Mr. J. Shyman Bell's words flew past it as quickly as the brown fields flew past the window and impressed themselves no more upon his *tabula* almost *rasa* than did the fleeting fields and trees upon the hazed pane of glass. Catholic Church, women's bicycles, well-built young ladies, they were but words and they passed to the nothingness out of which all words came and to which all words returned; and Mr. J. Shyman Bell was just an Englishfied blether who was talking through the seat of his pants.

"Yes," he said, his eyes more stupidly and more glintingly brown than ever, "but who *is* the Holy Ghost? Damn it, man, the Holy Ghost must be somebody if it can make a dancing hall fly onto the top of the Bass Rock. And what I should like to know is why there isn't a photograph of the Holy Ghost on the back page of the *Daily Mail* and not just snaps of my girls powdering their noses and looking like a lot of loose Lizzies. And not just a diddly, small wee photograph either. A large one." Mr. George Bleater pulled apart his hands as though he were playing a concertina. "A *large* one, a *very* large one so that people could see once and for all what the Holy Ghost looked like and wouldn't need to go round bothering ministers and clergymen and people."

"Yes," said Mr. J. Shyman Bell, doing his best to divert the conversation from the theological to the pornological, "these snaps of your little sweeties were yum-yum and no mistake." He saw, however, from the lack of expression in his companion's eyes that he was not ready to leave the Holy Ghost for the unholy living and so, producing a flask from the rabbit pocket on his generous backside, he handed it to Mr. George Bleater and said: "Another little drink wouldn't do us any harm, would it, Mr. George Bleater?"

Mr. George Bleater's eyes immediately lost their higher-things or their nothing-at-all look and, focusing themselves so hardly upon the flask that they almost squinted, sparkled and appeared to reflect more sunlight than a pale December sun was able to shine upon them.

"Well, perhaps a *small* one," he said, taking the flask and unscrewing the bright metal top. "Just a *very* small one." He filled the top which, when inverted, became a cup, to the brim, unconsciously illustrating the spiritual ecstasies described in the twenty-third psalm. "Ah," he said, polishing off the joy of the Lord at a single gulp, "that certainly does do a fellow a bit of good on a nasty cold morning like this."

"Now that's a true saying if ever there were one," said Mr. J. Shyman Bell, holding out his hand for the flask quite twenty seconds before Mr. George Bleater was ready to return it to him and filling the cup, when it was given to him, with splashing haste. "What I always say, Mr. George Bleater, is that religion's all very well in its way but that, when it comes down to a question of brass tacks, you can't beat a glass of whisky and stroking a pair of pretty legs. Of course, Mr. George Bleater, I am the last man in the world to do anything which—to do anything which Kipling would not have a true Englishman do but, like the other fellow, I must say that I like my little bit of fun occasionally. Nothing very wrong, you know, just a run in a car, a drink and a cuddle, and home to bye-byes. Now, that girl in your company, Mr. George Bleater, the one with the red hair and the big mouth, she looked as cute a little bit of goods as I've seen for many a long day. I don't suppose that *she* would be averse to having a little bit of fun occasionally, would she? Clean fun, of course, Mr. George Bleater, clean fun."

But Mr. George Bleater's eyes were glued upon the flask of whisky which Mr. J. Shyman Bell still held in his hand.

"Yes," he said. "That was good whisky all right."

"Like another one?"

"Well, perhaps just a *small* one. Just a *very* small one."

Once again Mr. J. Shyman Bell passed the flask and once again Mr. George Bleater poured himself out a good measure, pressed down and overflowing, and swallowed it and said "A-ah!" in an appreciative tone.

"Of course," he said, "Holy Ghost or no Holy Ghost, I'm going to tell this Father Whatever-he-calls-himself just what I think of him. I'm going to tell him straight that I think that he and his Holy Ghost had no business at all to land a lot of law-abiding folk on top of the Bass Rock at all hours of the night. And what the police think that they were up to I can't for the life of me imagine. But as I say, I am going to tell this Father Whatever-he-calls-himself just what I think of him and, what's more, I'm going to ask him for a refund of my out-of-pocket expenses."

"Quite," said Mr. J. Shyman Bell, taking back the flask and swigging at its contents almost as heartily as Mr. George Bleater had done. "And I, too, am going to call upon the same priest because, as I think that you will agree, the earning capacities of my dancing hall have been considerably damaged by its transference to the Bass Rock. Not that I believe in miracles, Mr. George Bleater. Please don't misunderstand me on that score. As that dean fellow says in the paper there, only the uneducated believe in miracles. But all the same you must admit that it's a bit thick when a superstitious priest removes a fellow's dancing hall to the top of the Bass Rock just to pretend that his rotten religion isn't all eye-wash."

"Yes," said Mr. George Bleater, "and I'm going to tell him just what I think of him and if he doesn't refund me my out-of-pocket expenses I'll know the reason why. Holy Ghost indeed! I'll give him Holy Ghost!"

And for the remainder of the journey the whisky flask, which was a large one, continued to pass backward and forward like an amber shuttlecock which wasn't quite certain at which end of its groove it ought to rest. So that, when the train steamed into the Waverley Station, Edinburgh, Mr. George Bleater was still pointing out that nobody had ever seen a photograph of the Holy Ghost and Mr. J. Shyman Bell was still speculating aloud as to the degree of clean fun which the chorus girl with the red hair and the large mouth would be willing to afford him and neither was listening to what the other was saying.

2.

LUNCH that day in the presbytery was a festive affair at which Canon

Geoghegan held out high hopes that the days of the modern novel, dancing, disbelief, and disorderly two-seaters were at an end and that the time was indeed ripe for the contemporary heathen—who were so much more hard-boiled than the real heathen in that they had had the Gospel preached unto them but had, from motives of sin or pseudo-science, rejected it—to submit their reason and their loins to the Church of God. And Father Neary had burbled over his third glass of beer that this time they had the disbelaivin' by the short hairs and that it would not be long before every stinkin' ould heretic in England was reconciled to the Holy Catholic Church. Father Malachy alone had taken no part in the general spiritual boisterousness and, as soon as he could decently do so, he excused himself and went into the church and, kneeling before the altar and, gazing upon the faded violet tabernacle curtains, which hid God in majesty and humility, he began to make his mid-day examination of conscience.

God was God, his mind told his soul as he shut his eyes to the hieratical upholstery around him, and had created man to love Him, to serve Him, and to be happy with Him forever. And because man had rebelled against God He had sent His Son, Who had been with Him since the timeless-less of time, to redeem His children and to found a Church which should unfailingly apply to all and for always the curative properties of His death and passion. And he, Malachy Murdoch, was a priest of this God and of this infallible Church (infallible because God, being God, could neither deceive nor be deceived) and it therefore behoved him to lead a life as free from blemish as it was possible for a human being to lead. He searched, then, in the familiar wastes of his soul for all those petty little sins of pride and cruelty which, because they are so petty and so little and so mean, do more to make people unhappy than all the lustings and the thievings and murderings which have splashed scarlet and crimson upon the centuries.

For behind the tabernacle door he knew, behind that faded violet curtain which he couldn't see, Jesus Christ lay cradled, as He had promised, in Bread until time should once more pass back to timelessness and Himself come to rout Anti-Christ, riding upon a cloud in great glory. And with Him, inseparable in Bread as in unity, lay God the Father and God the Holy Ghost, the Creator in the creature for the creature, the Power which had fashioned the world out of chaos and which could, were It but to put off the powerlessness which It had imposed upon Itself, shine forth and shatter to a million nothings that which Itself had created of one. In churches the world over, in neglected wayside chapels as in Saint Peter's, Rome, God, reduced to a flake of Himself, lay waiting for men to come and love Him. Surely, in face of a Love so great, it was impossible to let the soul rot and rust with petty prideful sins. So prying, prying went his mind, peering into this and peering into that, examining motive and weighing intention, striving to smooth out self into selflessness and to acquire that peace which comes only to those who do not seek it. And the faded violet curtains hung still and unseen before his eyes, strips of coloured silk cloaking eternity from time.

3.

ABOUT five minutes after Father Malachy had begun his examination of conscience, Mr. George Bleater and Mr. J. Shyman Bell, cocktailed, lunched, wined and liqueured, presented themselves at the door of the presbytery and asked to see "the priest who was responsible for all this miracle business." At first James, who had received strict instructions from Canon Geoghegan to allow no visitor who was not in Holy Orders to enter the house, had been all for refusing to admit them; but, on learning the identity of the spirituous callers, he had decided that they were the exceptions which proved the rule and, showing them into the small parlour usually reserved for interviews with potential converts, he shuffled off into the church to inform Father Malachy that two dhrunken divils of hiritics wanted to speak with him.

The parlour in which the two visitors found themselves was one of those bare rooms which, when consecrated to theological consultations, succeed in making the spiritual life seem ten times more unattractive than it actually is. The chairs had evidently been carpentered with the purpose of mortifying two out of the five senses and the walls, distempered in pale grey, were hung with pictures which represented, as Novemberishly as was possible, the cardinal archbishop of New York blessing a motor tractor, a certain Father Brannigan presenting a gold watch to the captain of the parish football team, Saint Ignatius rolling his eyes to heaven, Canon Geoghegan telling a famous cinema actress *de passage* in Edinburgh that films could be a source of great good and of great evil, and the Angel of the Lord, pink, chubby and anthropomorphic, appearing unto Mary.

"Don't think much of these gadgets," said Mr. J. Shyman Bell when he had walked round the room and stood and bleared at each picture. "Not very cheerful, what? And yet they say that these Roman Catholics are great boys for arty colouring and all that. Well, well. It just shows you that you can't believe everything you hear, doesn't it?"

Mr. George Bleater did not immediately reply for he, too, was inspecting the pictures and he was taking longer about it than Mr. J. Shyman Bell had done. At length, however, he had finished and, taking off his gold-rimmed pince-nez and wiping them energetically on his handkerchief, he remarked:

"I thought as much. No photograph of the Holy Ghost. Not a snap even. What I say is this: all these churchy people ought to be compelled by law to keep photographs of the Holy Ghost and then all this humbug would come to an end because they wouldn't be able to get hold of a photograph of the Holy Ghost. And why wouldn't they be able to get hold of a photograph of the Holy Ghost? Well, I'll tell you. Because the Holy Ghost is an imaginary imagination and even Bacon up there in Princes Street can't take a photo of an imaginary imagination." His big brown eyes flashed in confident wrath and he began to walk up and down the room with small, dumpy steps.

"Holy Ghost indeed. Damn it, man, who *is* the Holy Ghost? I've asked ministers and they can't tell me." And as he stumped up and down in his neat blue suit (he had left his overcoat in the hall) the very creases on the seat of his trousers seemed to express Erastianism, Machiavellianism, Joynson Hicksism and all the other sanities beloved by those who will have no priest between them and God.

"Now the sort of thing that I like," said Mr. J. Shyman Bell who was thoroughly tired of Mr. George Bleater and the Holy Ghost, "now the sort of thing that I like is something with a bit of a kick in it. They do these things so well in Paris, you know. Girls, I mean. Naughty but nice." His thumb and forefinger ceased scratching along their accustomed furrow and transferred themselves to one of his pockets from which they extracted the current issue of the *London Mail.* "Now, *that's* the sort of thing that brightens cricket," he said, pointing to an illustration of a young girl lying on a sofa in what a Nordic artist imagined a Nordic public would interpret as a state of abandon. "Cheers a fellow up after a hard day's work at the office. Whereas all this holy bunk—well, to be quite frank with you, Mr. George Bleater, I must confess that it gives me the pip in five places."

This time, however, the sudden and silent entry of Father Malachy prevented Mr. George Bleater from making an inconsequent reply; and with him there seemed to come some of the Benedictine peace, the shadow of that PAX which lies so surely over Solesmes, Farnborough, and Montserrat, the shadow of a reality which was nonetheless real for being itself a shadow. Even Mr. George Bleater seemed to sense the spiritual electricity in the air, for his eyes softened from wrath to stupidity and Mr. J. Shyman Bell, with a temporary blush spreading over his permanent one, hastily replaced the *London Mail* in his pocket and pulled down the flap so that the title should not be seen.

"I understand, gentlemen, that you wish to see me." Father Malachy's voice was quiet and steady as he uttered the simple sentence. "And may I ask the nature of your business?"

Now neither Mr. George Bleater nor Mr. J. Shyman Bell, for all that they knew more about the Catholic Church than the Pope of Rome did, had ever spoken to or been spoken to by a priest in their lives before; and the ordinariness of Father Malachy's voice astonished them so that they looked at each other in perplexity, moistened their lips with their tongues, coughed solemnly as though they were at a board meeting or a funeral, looked away again and changed, for something to do, the position of their feet.

"Perhaps," said Father Malachy, indicating the uncomfortable chairs, "you will be seated."

They sat down, taking a long time about it. For Mr. George Bleater had an eye on Mr. J. Shyman Bell and Mr. J. Shyman Bell had an eye on Mr. George Bleater, as neither wished to commit what the other might describe as a solecism. At last, however, they were seated and, as they leaned back against the creaking wood, Father Malachy sat down too and folded his hands in front of him.

"Was it by any chance about the miracle that you wished to see me?" he asked gently.

Once again Mr. George Bleater and Mr. J. Shyman Bell looked at each other in perplexity and once again they moistened their lips with their tongues; but this time Mr. George Bleater who, being a stupider man than his companion, feared the unknown less, said, lurchingly:

"Look here, Mister, it's all very well to talk about the Holy Ghost and all that, but what we want to know is..."

But he got no further, for Father Malachy was holding up his right hand, almost in the manner of the priest of the Lyceum stage forbidding a seduction, and saying:

"Excuse me, gentlemen. I am a monk and a priest; my title is 'Father,' Father Malachy Murdoch of the Order of Saint Benedict. A mere matter of form, I know, but if we didn't observe matters of form there would be even more strife and unpleasantness in the world than there actually is."

"I am sure, Father Malachy Murdoch, that Mr. George Bleater

joins me in proffering our most sincere apologies for any slight which we may have unconsciously offered you." Mr. J. Shyman Bell spoke slowly and sonorously, but not too slowly and not too sonorously, for he did not want Mr. George Bleater to interrupt him. "Perhaps when I tell you, Father Malachy Murdoch, that both Mr. George Bleater and myself are stout Protestants to whom the Faith that we learned at our mothers' knees is dearer than life itself, perhaps then you will understand that, having had no occasion for intercourse with Roman Catholic clergymen, we are naturally at a loss for words and terms. And, Father Malachy Murdoch, in view of the fact that one religion is as good as another and that one day we shall have to stand together before the All-Father and take our chances as man to man, in view of that fact, Father Malachy Murdoch, I am sure that you will forgive us." His beady little eyes were wet as he concluded, partly owing to his ante-prandial, prandial, and post-prandial bibbings, partly owing to the sincerity of his insincerity. "Yes, Father Malachy Murdoch, in view of that fact I am sure that you will forgive us."

Father Malachy bowed slightly.

"I understand perfectly," he said.

His tone seemed to imply so much more than the sentence which it cradled that Mr. George Bleater and Mr. J. Shyman Bell were again at a loss for words and for thoughts. And indeed Father Malachy himself, whose spiritual sensibilities were acute, did not quite know how to address his visitors, whom he realized to be a thousand years and a solar system of prejudices and environment distant from him. They sat, therefore, without speaking, outwardly three human beings looking at one another, inwardly three sets of metaphysics and moral philosophies packed up and hidden in bindings that were, to an unmental eye, the same. Three human beings: three universes, three cosmologies, three worlds, three Scotlands, three Spains, three rooms in which they sat, three units miserably failing to be one unity.

At length, however, Father Malachy asked again:

"Was it by any chance about the miracle that you wished to see me?"

Mr. J. Shyman Bell looked at Mr. George Bleater and saw that, given the opportunity, the other would obscure the issue by asking irrelevant questions about the Holy Ghost. He turned, therefore, to Father Malachy and said with energetic unctuousness:

"I do not know, Father Malachy Murdoch, if your servant informed you as to our identity. My friend here is Mr. George Bleater, manager of the *Whose Baby Are You?* company, the chorus of which was present at my invitation in the Garden of Eden on Saturday night. And I myself have the honour to be Mr. J. Shyman Bell, manager and owner of the Garden of Eden." He had been producing, as he talked, a card from his pocketbook and he handed it, with a flick and a flourish, to Father Malachy. "So I think that you will realize that we have some fairly sound reasons for being interested in your wonderful little miracle."

Father Malachy rose and held out his hand and Mr. George Bleater and Mr. J. Shyman Bell did likewise. Awkwardly, self-consciously the three worlds, the three Scotlands, the three Spains shook hands and made polite noises at one another and sat down again.

"And now," said Mr. J. Shyman Bell, who was beginning to recover his accustomed self-assurance, "and now that we have shaken hands like good men and true perhaps it will be easier for us to see eye-to-eye on the rather delicate matter which we have to discuss together."

Mr. George Bleater, to whom his companion's verbosity was distasteful, sat with a glower on his face and another in his mind. What, he refrained from asking, was the good of all this blethering and beating about the bush? Why not go straight to the point and ask the fellow bang out who the Holy Ghost was and whether he had any intention of paying for the damages caused by his hanky-panky? Perhaps the fellow had taken out an insurance policy for his miracles. These Roman Catholic priests were up to all sorts of dodges and nobody could tell what they'd be doing next. But, insurance policy or no insurance policy, all this havering about "delicate little matters" was sheer damned silliness.

"Yes," said Father Malachy, "the ways of Almighty God *are* delicate, aren't they? I often think that the world is like the shroud which wrapped Our Lord's Body when It was laid in the tomb: it bears His imprint in every mountain and valley."

Mr. J. Shyman Bell's face assumed that expression of expressionlessness which he deemed fitting to references about the glorious dead, his Saviour, and unintentional *double entendres* in the presence of ladies of principle.

"Quite," he said. "And these little matters, delicate, as we have both agreed, in themselves, are made more delicate because they can also be expressed in terms of a commodity which neither priest nor dance-hall proprietor, Father Malachy Murdoch, can live without."

"Yes," blustered Mr. George Bleater, "Saturday night's high jinks with your Holy Ghost cost me a little over a hundred pounds. A little over a hundred pounds, I tell you. And what for? Just to feed and lodge twenty-odd chorus girls whose nerves were shattered at suddenly finding themselves on the Bass Rock. It was no good my telling them that it was the Holy Ghost who had done it; they just laughed at me and told me that as their presence in the Garden of Eden was good publicity for my show they thought that I ought to pay for any misadventures which might happen to them in it. So I think that as it was you who asked the Holy Ghost to perform this queer sort of business, I think that it is only fair that you should stump up." He pulled a small piece of crumpled paper from his waistcoat pocket and looked at it angrily. "One hundred and thirteen pounds, nineteen shillings, that's what you owe me. And if you can't see your way to paying me I'll write a letter to the papers about it. Mind you, I mean what I say. I'll write letters to *all* the papers about it. Not just a *wee* letter, either; a *long* letter with full names. Damn it, man, I once prevented my next-door neighbour from keeping hens by writing to the papers about it. Yes, I mean what I say. I'll write to the papers about it unless you compensate me for the unlawful detention of my girls on the Bass Rock by the Holy Ghost."

Father Malachy, completely concealing his amazement and his disgust, said gently:

"Of course, Mr. Bleater, of course I shall compensate you in full. I had forgotten that miracles could be expressed in terms of money, but then I am only a very unbusinesslike monk and acquainted more with the philosophical than the practical problems of life. So you really must excuse me for not having realized that I should have to pay for my miracle. But as it has been such a good miracle I have no doubt that either the diocesan authorities or my own community at Fort William will be more than willing to reimburse you any sum by which you may find yourself poorer on its account."

"Cash," said Mr. George Bleater unashamedly, "hard, glittering spondulicks."

Father Malachy bowed.

"I understand perfectly and I think that I can guarantee that either the right reverend the lord bishop of Midlothian or the right reverend the lord abbot of Fort William will pay you the amount you claim in hard, glittering spondulicks."

Mr. J. Shyman Bell, who never asked a direct question if he could ask three indirect ones and who prided himself on commercial *finesse* and on being able to tell the right smutty story to the right patron at the right moment, was genuinely distressed by Mr. George Bleater's blundering descent to the brass tacks; and, seeing that the other was about to ask "When," he addressed himself immediately to Father Malachy.

"I am afraid, Father Malachy Murdoch," he began, "that you must excuse the somewhat abrupt manner in which my old pal Mr. George Bleater has chosen to express himself. When you've known old Geordie as long as I have you'll know that his bark is worse than his bite. Isn't that so, old man?" He switched, for a moment, the lighted turnip of his face upon his companion. "An old college chum of Geordie's once told me that he was so bad-tempered that he ought to have been a sergeant-major. Now, Geordie, don't lose your wool or I'll tell Father

Malachy Murdoch here all about your past." The lighted turnip was again shining full upon Father Malachy. "And of course, Father Malachy Murdoch, we must remember—must we not?—that he really has been considerably inconvenienced by this little miracle of yours and that he has still to catch a train to Newcastle this afternoon in order to be in time for the first performance tonight."

Looking at Mr. J. Shyman Bell's fat face and listening to his suave tones, Father Malachy was tempted to wonder if Almighty God could really have intended that he should love this man and see in him, naked or hungering, Christ naked, Christ hungering. And Saint John had written—had he not?—something like: "if a man love not his neighbour whom he hath seen, how shall he love God Whom he hath not seen?" Poor Saint John. He certainly could not have foreseen the bladder-like face of Mr. J. Shyman Bell, pre-created from all eternity for all eternity. But, with an effort, he brushed the cynicism from him and said: "You may rest assured, Mr. Bell, that I harbour no resentment against your friend for any asperity which there may have been in his mode of addressing himself to me."

"It is indeed good of you, Father Malachy Murdoch, to be so patient with us." Mr. J. Shyman Bell's thumb and forefinger began to dig periods out of his scar. "But perhaps you will permit me to say that I am not surprised because, being by nature a quick judge of character, I knew you, as soon as I saw you, Father Malachy Murdoch, to be the man you are. Now, as I think I have already told you, I am a stout Protestant and I would gladly suffer death rather than renounce those principles for which my Covenanting forefathers shed their glorious blood on our Scottish moors; and you are a devout Roman Catholic and no doubt you feel just the same way as I do about those higher things about which, when all is said and done, we shall know nothing for certain until we have passed into the Great Beyond. But we are both, I take it, men of the world and therefore I see no reason why we should not come to a satisfactory understanding about the—about the financial side of—of this very religious—of this very religious miracle which you have brought off. You have just, out of the kindness of your heart, which I am glad to see is clean and British, offered to refund to my friend Mr. George Bleater the expenses which he has incurred as a result of the aforesaid religious miracle. Now I also, Father Malachy Murdoch, am a loser in respect thereof and I estimate my losses at little short of a hundred thousand pounds."

"A hundred thousand pounds." Father Malachy repeated the amount over to himself. "To a poor monk like myself that sounds a great deal of money."

"It *is* a great deal of money, Father Malachy Murdoch. But it is no more than I have lost or stand to lose through your removal of my dance hall from its former site. A dance hall on the top of the Bass Rock, Father Malachy Murdoch, is something of a white elephant; and plain businessmen, however deep and sincere their respect for religious miracles, cannot afford to lose buildings, fittings, and fixtures, good will, earning capacity and all, without claiming some pecuniary compensation in return."

Oh dear, thought Father Malachy, but what a fool he had been. He might have realized that one just couldn't go borrowing dance halls for the purpose of proving the eternal verities without having to pay the owners. And Canon Geoghegan. And the bishop. The idea hadn't seemed to strike them either. And Almighty God. Almighty God had allowed him to perform the miracle and had not permitted the Holy Ghost to inspire him with any counsels of prudence. Which meant that Almighty God was all for the miracle. Which meant that the money would be found somewhere. He smiled again in his soul and from his soul.

"Mr. Bell," he said, "I must be frank with you. I don't know at the moment how or where I am going to find so large a sum of money as you have just mentioned. But I fully realize that you are entitled to compensation for the losses which you have sustained through this very wonderful manifestation of God's power and I ask you to believe that, had the practical side of the question crossed my mind, I would have formally asked your permission before attempting the miracle. I have said that I don't know where I am going to find the money, but I am certain that it will be found. Perhaps the bishop of Midlothian will find it for me, perhaps my abbot, perhaps we shall have to open a subscription fund. But one thing I do know, Mr. Bell: and that is that Almighty God will find a way to reimburse you for the loss of your dancing hall."

"Yes," said Mr. J. Shyman Bell. "Yes, Father Malachy Murdoch, but supposing He doesn't?"

"But He will. He allowed the miracle to be performed. Therefore He will find the money to pay for it. It's really very simple."

Mr. J. Shyman Bell was not too sure about God finding the money, but he realized that to stress his skepticism would be tactless.

"Father Malachy Murdoch," he said, "since you have been generous, I'll be generous, too. If you get the—the Holy Ghost, wasn't it?—if you get the Holy Ghost to bring back my dance hall in time for tonight's evening session I shan't claim a penny from you. Perhaps that will be the simplest way out of the difficulty and we'd both be satisfied. Yes, Father Malachy Murdoch, get the Holy Ghost to bring back the Garden of Eden and we'll cry quits."

"I am afraid that you don't quite understand the position," Father Malachy explained. "I asked Almighty God to allow me to perform this miracle in order that unbelievers and heretics might be confounded. And, as miracles aren't believed in in a day, unbelievers and heretics will not be confounded in a day. No, Mr. Bell, your dance hall has got to go on sitting on the Bass Rock until the world comes back to faith in Our Blessed Lord. And that, as I have said, will not be in a day. You yourself, Mr. Bell. You come here to claim damages because I have removed your dance hall to the Bass Rock and yet you don't really believe in the miracle. Not really and truly and without mental reservations."

"I have told you that I am a stout Protestant," Mr. J. Shyman Bell defended.

"Even stout Protestants must accept the evidence of their eyes. Saint Thomas, if you will pardon my saying so, was well on the way to becoming a stout Protestant until he thrust his hand in Our Lord's side." The sigh in Father Malachy's spirit billowed out into his voice. "But I forgot. You did not come here for a course of dogmatic theology, did you? You came here seeking lawful damages which you have very kindly offered to forego if I annul my miracle by performing another and reinstate your dance hall where it was before. Well, my answer to that is that I cannot reinstate your dance hall but that I am perfectly prepared to approach my ecclesiastical superiors with regard to the money which you claim. And that, gentlemen, is, I am afraid, all that I can say or do for the moment."

And, after a few other courtesies had been exchanged between Mr. J. Shyman Bell and Father Malachy, they all took leave of one another and returned to their separate worlds; Mr. George Bleater to two large whiskies and the afternoon train to Newcastle; Mr. J. Shyman Bell to the Braid Hills and a little bit of fluff he had picked up in the lounge of the new picture house; and Father Malachy to the solemn *Te Deum* in front of what had once been the Garden of Eden, sung by the bishop and Canon Geoghegan and himself, the three of them in their snappiest white vestments.

4.

HALF an hour later, after having intoned the *Te Deum* in the presence of an odd ten thousand centres of the universe (which included a bewildered thirty, of the all-for-morning-prayer-but-never-at-it kindergarten of thought, from the adjacent Stock Exchange) the bishop, Canon Geoghegan, and Father Malachy were unvesting in the sacristy and, as the bishop, snuffling and sniffling, was trying to disentangle his pectoral cross from his stole, a meaningless rhyme, composed by him when a novice, was running through Father Malachy's head:

"Father Time
Was at Prime;
But at None
He was gone."

At last, however, the bishop had freed pectoral cross from stole and stole from pectoral cross and, standing gaunt and gawky and looking, in his unornamented alb, like the farmer of farce in the nightgown of farce, was mumbling:

"Ah saw Aundry in the crowd. With his wee bit hen as he calls her. His wee bit hen. Och, well, Aundry was always a bit of a coamic."

Canon Geoghegan did not answer. He regarded the sacristy as the direct antechamber to the sanctuary and had forbidden his curates to indulge in secular tittle-tattle while vesting or unvesting. But the bishop was the bishop; and one could show disapproval only by silence when he broke rules and rubrics or bungled his ritual at Pontifical High Mass.

"Aye," said the bishop, who secretly thought that Canon Geoghegan was a bit of an auld fusspot, "aye and his wee bit hen seemed to me to be more like a wee bit bubbly-jock than a wee bit hen. She was wearing one of yon coloured sweaters that look just like a rainbow with the measles. Aye, aye." His voice became more of a mumble than ever as he pulled his alb over his head. "Aye," he said again as he began to unbutton his cassock, "Ah suppose Ah'd better be getting home for ma tea."

"If your lordship will excuse me," Father Malachy broke in, "I'd like to have a word with you before you go home."

"Of course Ah'll excuse you and you can have as many wurrds with me as you like." The bishop was feeling more genial than he had ever felt since the day when he had preached, at the opening of the convent school for girls and *coran cardinali* and prominent heretics, on the "Flames o' Hell as a Speeritual and Pheesical Reality." "And wasn't all yon crowd just the finest thing ye ever saw? All the godless lassies and laddies who think only of theeters and pictures. Well, all that Ah can say is that yon miracle of yours has given them pictures. Man, Malachy, Ah shouldn't be surprised if you and your Garden of Eden were to convert the whole world from Dan to Beersheba and from John O' Groat's to Bewnos Airs."

"Perhaps your lordship would prefer to interview Father Malachy in the house," Canon Geoghegan suggested.

"And perhaps ma lordship would prefer to have a wee bit confabulation just where we are. What say you, Father Malachy? We're fine where we are, aren't we?"

But the debt of a hundred thousand pounds was beginning to appear so large to Father Malachy that he was unable to smile.

"My lord," he said, "in the early part of the afternoon I received a visit from a Mr. J. Shyman Bell who stated that he was the owner of the Garden of Eden."

"Ye did, did ye? And what might he be wanting? Has he been converted or what?"

"I'm afraid not, my lord. All that he seems to be wanting is a hundred thousand pounds for his dance hall."

"A hundred thousand pounds. Why did he no make it a million when he was about it? And we haven't stolen his dance hall, have we? All that we've done is to flit it to the Bass Rock."

"That is so, my lord; but Mr. Bell points out that this removal of the Garden of Eden to the Bass Rock is as good as theft because it has turned it from a profit-earning establishment into a structural curiosity. And, while in no way sympathizing with Mr. Bell's philosophy of life, I must really say that I admit the justice of his claim. Indeed, so convinced was I of the reality of his losses that I undertook to approach you and my abbot with a view to seeing how the money could be found."

"That was kind of ye. But I haven't got a hundred thousand pence, let alone a hundred thousand pounds." The bishop was by now out of his cassock and into his clerical coat and was appearing not at all pontifical. "But in any case the laddie'll have to justify his claim: buildings so much, fancy carpets so much, what-nots so much, electric fittings so much. And he can't do that in under a month—not justify it, I mean. And by that time we may have converted a few of yon wealthy fellows who live out by in Murrayfield and never darken a church door. Dinna fash yerself, Malachy; the money side of the business will settle itself."

"Yes," said Canon Geoghegan, "and in any case our Protestant friends are for the moment disbelieving so faithfully in the miracle that they will find it difficult to treat it as real or to have it treated as real for legal purposes. Yes, for once I rather think I am sorry for our Protestant friends." He smiled in a semi-Oriental manner, as though to indicate that Protestants were his friends only for rhetorical purposes. (For when Canon Geoghegan made use of the phrase "our Protestant friends" one felt that he would have liked to be able to dispense with diplomatic flatulence and to call them roundly effing bees; but then the Reverend Dr. Montrose McMichen, who had preached on several occasions before the King in Crathie parish church, always gruffed out "our Western brethren" just as though he meant it to sound like effing cees.) "Yes, this time I think that our Protestant friends have bitten off more than they can chew."

"But," Father Malachy protested, "the poor man is entitled to some pecuniary compensation. We know that the miracle is a true one and we know that he has been deprived of his lawful means of livelihood because of the miracle. Therefore it is our duty to pay Mr. Bell any sum which he may justifiably claim."

"The man's means of livelihood was not lawful," Canon Geoghegan intoned. "The Garden of Eden was an iniquitous blot upon the parish and the diocese, and its removal to the Bass Rock is in the nature of a personal subscription from the Catholic Church towards Scottish purity."

"I maintain, Canon, that you are grossly exaggerating the true state of affairs." Father Malachy spoke with patience and kindness.

"And I also maintain that, economically and morally, we are bound to make some restitution to Mr. Bell for the commerce of which we have deprived him."

"And *I* maintain that the sins practised in and because of the Garden of Eden relieve us from the obligation to make any restitution. This Mr. Bell must be a very gross personage from what I have heard of him, and the souls which he has caused to be damned deny him the right to plead any cause against us." The canon was flushed and angry. "And, if we *did* make any restitution, the Garden of Eden would become our property. And what would we do with it? Turn it into a summer house for the children of Mary?"

"We could turn it into a church where monks would perpetually sing the office in gratitude to Almighty God for the miracle. And that is another reason why we should make restitution, Canon. We must at all costs prevent this building, which has been so marvellously used by God, from being desecrated by secular hands."

The bishop reached for his black felt hat and said snotteringly:

"Have your little argy-bargy if you must; but Ah'm awa' hame for ma tea."

And, after allowing Canon Geoghegan and Father Malachy to kiss his ring, the lord bishop of Midlothian passed out of the sacristy, through the church, across the street and into a tram where, producing his breviary and poring over it, he looked once more like the plain man's misconception of him: a Presbyterian minister who was indecently and unsportingly attached to Holy Writ.

CHAPTER VIII

1.

Two days passed, three; and Father Malachy's miracle had become the leading topic of conversation in every drawing room, office, bar, and railway carriage in the world.

The British had for so long allowed themselves to believe outwardly in a religion which they believed inwardly to be untrue that this public proof of the validity of its doctrines struck them as being in very bad taste and liable to damage trade. Faith, English faith, had always been a nice, neo-Gothic mist in which unattractive women and men who were bad at games could hide themselves and where their more human brothers and sisters could join them for religious Ascots, Derbys, and twelfths of August. And now here was a Roman Catholic monk proving that Christian doctrine was as much a fact as India or the Panama Canal. Well, well, if Christianity was as true as all that, they weren't going to believe in it any longer, not they.

Of course, they did not really reason like that—not explicitly, at any rate; but the sum total of their false deductions derived from falser premises amounted to the general conclusion that Christianity was all very well and healthy and English if it restricted itself to being a probable improbability but that it was an absolute washout if it started becoming unashamedly and obviously true. The scholarly utterances of popular deans and the private lives of abnormal actresses had done their work. Men and women who never read anything more profound than the report of a boxing match or a society wedding had now come to have intellectual difficulties in believing what Saint Ignatius Loyola, Saint Dominic, and Saint Benedict had swallowed without effort; and sin—fornication and adultery being now regarded as feats as intellectual as reading Tolstoy in the original—had proved such a pleasant alternative to golf in wet weather that it was not likely that clean-limbed English men and women were going to take more kindly to myth and mystery because they had become, for a week at least, fact and reality.

The thinkers and those who were able to choose their own library books and to ask for a cup of coffee in comprehensible French were, of course, dead against the miracle which they opposed as bitterly and as incompetently as Gladstone had, in the nineteenth century, opposed the biology of Darwin and Huxley. "Agnosticism," they declaimed from their pulpits and editorial chairs, "agnosticism has been for fifty years or more the only religious philosophy possible to the educated man and woman; and any attempt to justify, by a juggling that is as anachronous as it is clumsy, a supernaturalism repugnant to the intelligent mind is doomed to failure."

There were also, however, the naturally pious, those ultra-spiritual souls who were as ready to ascribe the receipt of an unexpected postal order to God as their opponents were to interpret High Mass in terms of Freud. Every day Leith Walk publicans, who recited daily twice as many rosaries as they sold bottles of champagne, knelt on the pavement of the vanished Garden of Eden and asked Our Lady to obtain them pardon for their spiritual apathy; and ladies of title and servant girls (in Scotland Catholicism is more or less confined to the social extremes) could be seen bowed in prayer and meditation before those once worldly railings. The High Church Anglicans, too, always ready to believe when a papist might, with good conscience, doubt, had shown great devotion to the miracle; and the Reverend Denis Meaty had called personally on the priests of the Church of Saint Margaret of Scotland and, after asking Canon Geoghegan how he disposed of his spectacles at the consecration, had confided that his own bishop was most interested in the miracle but, for fear of giving offense to the more timid and conservative souls committed to his charge, had to content himself with being interested at a distance.

Seductions, rapes, murders, and transatlantic flights were, as has already been indicated, scarce; and, as it was at least a fortnight before Scotland met France at Murrayfield, the miracle had as much honour in its own country as it had in Mexico, and it became quite the convention for sweet young things to talk, as they promenaded Princes Street, of how amusing it would be if religion and all that were really and truly true.

2.

On the Friday morning within the first octave of the miracle, Father Malachy, tired by constant interviews, was again informed by James that someone wished to see him in the parlour. He did not sigh but wished that he could have done so without forfeiting a particle of God's grace. (He had returned to his room only ten minutes ago from interviewing a female member of the British Fascisti who had prefaced her volubility by the request: "Please, Father, tell me all about religion"; and before that he had been instructing a chartered accountant, an international authority on columnar cash books, who stated that he had audited theology and found it correct.)

His new visitor turned out to be a prosperous-looking man of about fifty years of age, who was wearing a heavy black overcoat with a fur collar and who seemed to smell of cigar smoke, reminiscently, like a church of incense.

"Good morning," he boomed out straight away. "You're Father Malachy Murdoch, are you? Well, I've come to buy the rights of your miracle."

"I beg your pardon." Father Malachy, all huddled in his black cloak, seemed to be hugging himself for astonishment.

"I forgot. Of course, you don't know who I am. How very stupid of me." The stranger smiled and produced his card and handed it to Father Malachy. "As you will read, my name is Thomas Ink. Thomas B. Ink. Not entirely unknown, as I think you will agree."

Father Malachy studied the card attentively.

"You must pardon me, Mr. Ink," he said politely, "but, living as I do in a monastery, I am naturally somewhat out of touch with the outer world. Your name is certainly familiar to me; but whether you are known for exporting Protestant Bibles to South America or for plain and unsectarian horticulture, I can't for the life of me say."

Mr. Ink laughed, loudly and deeply.

"Unsectarian horticulture! Damned good. I can see that you and I are going to understand each other perfectly. No, I am afraid that I am known for neither of the rather dull accomplishments which you have just mentioned. Indeed, my profession is anything but a dull one. For I am, you see, a showman; and I think that I may, with all modesty, claim to be Britain's leading showman. At any rate, I have discovered more Spanish beauties and been bankrupt oftener than any of my rivals. In 1919 I staged *Put Me To Bye-Byes,* which ran six months longer than any other revue of its type, and was responsible for the successful filming of Miss Primrose Field's emotional little masterpiece *Mothers of Tomorrow.* In 1920 I organized three unsuccessful transatlantic flights, a crash on Wall Street, the *début* of Miss Trixie Tantana and the publicity work of the Lambeth Conference. In 1921, yes, in 1921,I failed for exactly double the amount of hundreds of thousands that any other showman has failed for. But in 1922 I was on my feet again and produced *Get Me, Girlie?* in the West End and Handel's *Messiah* in Birmingham and Glasgow and dined, if I remember rightly, with the ex-Kaiser at Doorn. In 1923 I financed two of the prize fights which made Chicago the metropolis of the ring and in 1924 I was again down and out. In 1925—but I need weary you no further, need I? I am sure that I have told you enough about myself for you to understand that I am a man of considerable action. And, my dear Father, the fact that you, essentially a man of inaction, have within the space of a single week attracted to yourself more publicity than I have in a lifetime—well, Father, all that I can say is that I am intrigued. For, whereas my name is familiar enough wherever English is spoken, yours is just as much a household word in Moscow as it is in Haiti."

Father Malachy bowed.

"Won't you sit down?" he asked. "I don't know about you, Mr. Ink, but I am very tired. As perhaps you can understand, I have been having rather a large number of callers these last few days."

Mr. Ink sat down and so did Father Malachy. "Well," said Mr. Ink, "as man to man, what's the trick?"

"The trick? I am afraid, Mr. Ink, that I don't quite understand you."

"Oh, yes, you do." Mr. Ink was jolly and confidential and twinkling. "Oh, yes, you do. I asked you to tell me as man to man, didn't I? Perhaps I ought to have put it more delicately and more aptly. As showman to showman, as celestial showman to terrestrial showman, what's the trick? In other words, how did you do it?"

Father Malachy appeared to become more grey and monkish and impersonal as he listened to his visitor.

"I presume that you are referring to my translation of the Garden of Eden to the Bass Rock?" he asked.

"Exactly. You see, I am interested professionally: firstly, in your technique; secondly, in the commercial possibilities of your miracle. And then I am unfortunate enough to be the largest shareholder in a music hall in Leeds which would pay much better if it could be removed to Bradford. So that, professionally, personally, and in every kind of way, I have been most impressed by your performance of last Saturday night." The merriment went from Mr. Ink's face and was replaced by an intense expression which was intended to convey such sentiments and policies as honesty, friendliness, and no Home Rule for India. "And I need hardly say, Father, that you would not be the loser by any services which you chose to render me."

"I think, Mr. Ink, that you and I are not at all likely to understand each other. My miracle was not a trick; it was a direct supervention of the supernatural, of which the purpose was and is to bring an apathetic and godless generation back to religion and right living. And"—Father Malachy smiled ever so slightly—"as Almighty God is more likely to disapprove than to approve your purposes, I am afraid that, even were I to choose to come to your aid, your music hall would continue to sit in Leeds."

Mr. Ink was puzzled and looked it. A frown rippled across his brow and spread, in dribbles, to the corners of his eyes.

"But," he protested uncertainly, "I thought that—that even religious people had given up believing in that sort of thing. And only last night the Protestant bishop of Wallington stated that it was not by upsetting the laws of physics that Christianity would commend itself to thoughtful people."

Father Malachy's smile broadened.

"My dear Mr. Ink," he said, "I am sorry to be forced to tell you that you are a sentimentalist. Belief makes no difference to fact. If all the people in the world were suddenly to go insane and to refuse to believe that the Channel Islands existed, the Channel Islands would still continue to lie where they do. And the same holds good with regard to abstract principles: two and two will continue to make four even if all the mathematicians in the world decide that, in accordance with modern thought, they ought to make five. Similarly the Trinity and the supernatural continue to crown physics and the natural in spite of what prominent heretical bishops and cinema actresses may believe to the contrary. Theology, Mr. Ink, is an exact science often misinterpreted as a sentimental opinion just as geology is often a sentimental opinion misinterpreted as an exact science."

Mr. Ink's expression of bewilderment changed to one of uneasiness. He had never pretended to understand the fuss that parsons and priests made about matters which, in his opinion, were best left alone. Religion was all very well when it confined itself to preserving ancient cathedrals and to marrying and burying people; but when it began to try to stop you from making love when and with whom you liked and to pretend to be true... He was almost on the point of taking his leave when he remembered that, miracle or fraud, there was money in this business and that, according to his trainer's last report, it was not likely that Cami-Knickers would win next year's Derby.

"I perceive, Father Malachy, that you are both a philosopher and a man of principle. Please, then, accept my sincerest apologies if I have said anything to offend you and believe that I entertain only sentiments of good will and admiration towards the cause of which you are so able an exponent." He made a heavy little bow, pulled half of it back again, and replaced it by a real Rotarian smile. "Let us, then, leave aside the—the more solemn aspects of this miracle of yours and talk, as even the most unworldly men must on occasion, business. Are you willing to sell the rights of your miracle? Perhaps the fact has not struck you, but your miracle has a certain cash value. And I have no doubt that you, like many other worthy clergymen, would be only too willing to earn a little extra money to enable you to carry on your great and noble work of aiding our less fortunate brothers and sisters."

Father Malachy thought of Mr. George Bleater and of Mr. J. Shyman Bell and of their claims and of the way that the bishop had seemed inclined to let the justice of God be tempered by the justice of men.

"It is not a *little* extra money that I require," he said. "It is a great deal of money. Yes, a great deal of money. Much more than you would be willing to give me, in all probability. But perhaps you would be good enough to tell me exactly in what, commercially speaking, the rights of my miracle consist."

"Cinema and serial," said Mr. Ink, without hesitation. "Dramatic, perhaps, although I am inclined to think that your miracle would make neither a good play nor a popular musical comedy. Of course, with a little human interest added..."

"And what exactly am I to understand by human interest?" Father Malachy asked.

Mr. Ink began to roll between his teeth the cigar which he wasn't smoking.

"Well, I'll tell you. In the first place, you'd have to drop all this stuff about performing your miracle to prove that your religion was truer than anybody else's. The great heart of the people wouldn't stand for it; and it's the great heart of the people, Father Malachy, and not their soul or their intellect which we showmen have to consider. Now, this miracle of yours would make a first-class talkie and it would be a great draw if you could play in it yourself. But real, human interest, remember, and no probing into this, that, and the other thing. The average mental age of any cinema audience is seventeen, Father, and the mind of seventeen is more concerned with love than religion. That's it; we'd have to give your miracle a love interest."

"But it has one already," Father Malachy protested. "Haven't I told you that I performed the miracle for the love of God?"

Mr. Ink brushed away the higher motives with an imperious wave of his imaginary cigar.

"I said seventeen, Father, not seventy. At seventeen people are concerned with loving—and in a strictly technical manner at that—each other and not with loving God. You'd have to be a monk who was always keen on praying in chapels and tending roses until one day you looked from out an old world turret window and saw a lover and his lass kissing each other with passionate abandon against an ivy-covered wall. It would come over you all of a sudden that human love is a very beautiful thing and that men and women were doing the work of the devil in shutting themselves up in monasteries and convents and flying from an emotion that was stronger than the iron bridge which spans the river and at the same time more tender than broken moonbeams falling on a forest lake. One might even show you, forty years younger, fleeing from a love that you were too cowardly to embrace. 'Your golden hair, Gretchen,' you would say, 'will always be a rope to bind my heart to the great something which men must always seek and never find; but, alas! my father is adamant and a monk I must be. Fare thee well, golden Gretchen; each year when the roses bloom I will think of thee.' Anyway, next day as you are walking along a lane, you meet the girl you saw kissing and being kissed and you are surprised to see that she is weeping bitterly. 'What ails thee, my daughter?' you ask in a voice that is both saintly and kind. 'My mother wants me to become a nun,' the fair young thing will answer, raising a tear-stained face to yours. 'And I, wretched creature that I am, love Fritz Ausenheim, who lives by yonder watermill.' 'Blaspheme not, daughter,' you will say, raising your hand in sweet reproof. 'Your love for Fritz Ausenheim is a very beautiful gift from God. Go, tell your mother that a poor monk desires speech with her.' You will then see the mother who will be a harsh, unattractive woman who is always worshipping the Virgin and bullying the servants. 'Get thee behind me, Satan,' she will say in answer to your request that her daughter be allowed to love and marry. 'Griselda is promised to the abbess of Saint-Mary-of-the-Mountain and to the abbess of Saint-Mary-of-the-Mountain she will go.' 'It is a shame and a sin to flout true love,' you will cry, nothing daunted by her flashing eyes, and you will transfer her baronial castle to the top of Mont Blanc until she sanctions the marriage of her daughter with Fritz Ausenheim—who will turn out to be the cobbler's or the blacksmith's son—and admits that true love is God's sunshine for human souls. The whole action to take place in the Austrian Tyrol."

Father Malachy was gently rocking with laughter by the time that Mr. Ink had finished.

"Do you really think that we're like that, Mr. Ink? Monks and priests, I mean. Dear, dear, but I think I know more about showmen than you do about monks. Seventeen, you said, Mr. Ink, didn't you? Well, in my opinion, the appeal of your film would be limited to badly instructed children of five."

Mr. Ink was hurt but did his best not to appear so.

"I admit," he said, "that there is nothing very profound in the plot which I have just outlined to you. But I think that my experience as a showman justifies me in preferring my own opinion to yours; and it is most decidedly my opinion that the public would lap up a first-class talkie planned on the lines I have just described."

"Well, in any case, I am afraid that I shall have to decline that particular proposal. My abbot would never give me permission to act in any film, let alone a film to propagate cheap and vulgar heterodoxy. No, I'm afraid that you'll have to think of something else, Mr. Ink. And please think of it quickly because I am very anxious to earn a nice fat sum of money."

Mr. Ink scratched his head, symbolically almost.

"There's the Sunday papers," he said at length. "A series of articles from your pen would be worth a mint of money; and I think that I know just the quarter in which they'd be most appreciated. Only once again, Father Malachy, you'd have to provide the human interest. And, after all, why shouldn't you? Hang it all, that dean fellow who's so down on your miracle was writing only a month ago in the *Sunday Rapid* on 'Should Girls Wear Garters?' "

Father Malachy shook his head.

"I decline to write about garters when I can write about souls," he said.

Mr. Ink thought. After all, there *was* a good deal of talk about religion in the papers these days. Charwomen, novelists, public schoolboys were always adding their trickle to the public diarrhoea of diluted theology. Yes, but this Malachy wouldn't dilute *his* theology. That was just the trouble. He would treat religion as though it were as important as cricket or aëronautics. Yet the whole point of his miracle, according to him, was that religion was more important than cricket or aëronautics and the public would certainly be interested to hear the miracle-monger's views on his own miracle. It was just possible that the time was ripe for religion to rake in as much money as legs. This priest was certainly—for the moment, at least—famous enough to command any price he chose for his public utterances, written or spoken; and it was likely to be a very long time before another opportunity for exploiting religion would occur. Yes, perhaps it would be best to give him *carte blanche* as regards his subject and his treatment of it.

"What do you say to four consecutive and exclusive articles in the *Sunday Messenger* and lectures in London, Birmingham, Liverpool, Manchester, Glasgow, and this rather noble architectural hiccup which has the temerity to proclaim itself a capital?" Mr. Ink was as suave and as ultimately thirteen-second-Corinthians in charity as he had been when he had persuaded Miss Dillie Delaney to appear in Singapore without a *cache-sexe*. "Eh, what do you say to that?"

Father Malachy answered, readily enough:

"Three things: firstly, that you give me time to obtain the permission of my abbot; secondly, that I may speak of my miracle as I believe that Almighty God would have me speak of it; and thirdly, that you pay to me the sum of one hundred thousand, one hundred and thirteen pounds, nineteen shillings."

"One hundred thousand, one hundred and thirteen pounds, nineteen shillings is both a large sum and a curious sum," Mr. Ink murmured reflectively. "May I be so indiscreet as to ask you if you have any special reason for naming it?"

"I have a very special reason," said Father Malachy, "but, if you don't mind, I rather think that I shall keep it to myself. One hundred thousand, one hundred and thirteen pounds, nineteen shillings is my price, Mr. Ink, for telling the British public what it ought to know already."

"Of course," said Mr. Ink, "you'll have to give me time to approach newspaper proprietors and the owners of large public halls. And, as I cannot afford to be a loser over this transaction, I shall have to satisfy myself that our gross receipts will be sufficient to pay you the sum you have demanded after allowing for general expenses and my little commission."

"That is entirely your affair, Mr. Ink. And, as long as the result of your labours will be to guarantee me one hundred thousand, one hundred and thirteen pounds, nineteen shillings, I shall ask to know nothing more. And, on your part, you must give me sufficient time to communicate with my abbot."

"Of course," said Mr. Ink, rising. "Of course, Father Malachy. Then perhaps in a couple of days or so from now we might meet again? We must strike while the iron's hot, you know." And, finding conversation difficult now that business had been exhausted, he remarked, in spite of the gay sunshine outside: "Rotten weather, is it not?"

3.

YES, thought Father Malachy, as he mounted to his room, Almighty God wasn't going to let him down after all. The abbot mightn't altogether like the idea of the newspaper articles and the popular lectures, but he couldn't very well object in view of the publicity that would be obtained for Catholic orthodoxy. And Mr. George Bleater and Mr. Shyman Bell would be paid in full and the Garden of Eden would become a basilica where converted Britons would do penance for three and a half centuries of pig-headedness. Yes, yes, you could always trust Almighty God; He wasn't the sort of Person to perform a miracle and then let it get messed up for want of one hundred thousand, one hundred and thirteen pounds, nineteen shillings, not He. He just reversed the principle of one of His own parables and made unto Himself friends of the mammon of unrighteousness that *He* might receive *them* into *His* dwellings. Dear old Almighty God; He was a one, He was.

CHAPTER IX

1.

THAT same Friday the afternoon and evening papers were as full of miracle and metaphysic as they were ordinarily full of horse-racing and adultery. A few spineless aesthetes had, it appeared, been converted and had asked the competent authorities to receive them into the Church of Rome; but such, as the press took pains to point out, were for the most part disloyal members of the Church of England, whose superstitious mummeries had long been condemned by representative thinkers like Lord Brentford and the bishop of Birmingham. The great mass of the people was still unconvinced of the reality of the miracle and leader writers were confident that a thing called British sanity would win another thing called the day. Scotland, especially, was not going to be false to her ancient traditions and that very afternoon, at a united anti-miracle meeting, an eminent local Luther had preached (S.B. to all stations): "O God, Who art surrounded by cherubime and seraphime, deliver us from all drunkards, breakers of the Sabbath, whoremongers, and Roman Catholics."

Such, at any rate, were the facts which Mr. J. Shyman Bell gleaned from the Edinburgh *Evening Messenger* propped, like a groggy altar card, against the mirror of his dressing table. Yes, he argued as he began tying his black tie for the fifth time, yes, the papers were right. British sanity would win the day. Miracles simply didn't happen; and sooner or later the thing would be exposed for the hoax that it was. And, even if the real truth of the matter were never known, he would always get that hundred thousand for the wrongful removal of his dancing hall. If necessary, he would take the matter to court; a popish priest wouldn't stand an earthly before an honest Scottish judge. Not that it was at all likely that he would be forced to take proceedings. Fear of his own skin would make the priest pay up, fear of being shown up for the impostor that he was. And on the interest from a hundred thousand pounds he and Bella could live like a couple of fighting cocks and get slewed up every night of the week if they wanted to.

"Nearly ready?" he called through the open door to the bedroom where his hardboiled wife, kilted in white underclothes, was polishing her nails.

"Almost, Jimmy." Her voice was the querulous wail of a woman to whom fashionable hotels, champagne, and jazz are the ultimate beatitudes. "Dear, but I do wish we hadn't to go and dine with these beastly Succoths."

"I know, Bella, I know. A bore, of course." He was silent as he fumbled intricately with his tie. "But these little social duties have got to be done. And the Succoths, remember, are one of the most wealthy and cultured families in Murrayfield."

"I think that Alastair Succoth looks more like a tram conductor than a stockbroker. That thin, measly, peasly face of his." She probed with her nail file as though the quick on her finger were the thin, measly, peasly face of Alastair Succoth. "And, as for his wife, she's the most stuck-up woman in Edinburgh. I'm not so sure, either, that she hasn't got lovers. Not that I'd blame her for that. I know jolly well that I shouldn't like to have to be pawed about by Alastair Succoth."

"Still," said Mr. J. Shyman Bell, patting peace to his tie and reaching for his waistcoat, "still, it doesn't do us any harm socially to know these people. Succoth's got a lot of influence in the right quarter. A member of Muirfield and all that. He might be useful to us some day. You never can tell."

There was a rustling as Mrs. Shyman Bell poured a crimson and silver frock over herself.

"And another thing," she said, "they'll be asking us all about that bloody miracle."

"Yes, Bella, I suppose they will."

"Well, if they do, I've a good mind to tell them straight out that it's none of their business. I'm just about fed up with that miracle. Only this afternoon Mrs. Mackenzie stopped me in Princes Street and asked me if I thought it was the Lord Jesus Christ or the Devil who had removed our dance hall. I nearly told her—oh, I don't know what I nearly told her; but I was so angry that I almost spat in her face."

"Poor Bella."

Mrs. J. Shyman Bell gave some final pulls and tugs to her frock and, gazing at her reflection in the glass, decided that she looked at least five years younger than she actually was.

"Oh, well," she said, "I hope to God they give us something decent to drink."

2.

At that very moment Mr. and Mrs. Succoth, dressed for dinner, were sitting in the smoke room of what transatlantic captionists would have called their luxurious Murrayfield home. They were drinking a preliminary cocktail and Nora Succoth, who was twenty-seven and was looking very worldly in a wispy black frock, said on a little wind of alcohol:

"God, Alastair, but whatever made you want to invite swine like that I can't for the life of me imagine."

Alastair Succoth picked at his pseudo-military moustache. He was a man of about thirty-five years of age and had become a stockbroker because his father had made money in machine tools and because there were "no bally exams, to pass." He owned an Isotta-Fraschini, lunched every day in the grill room of the North British Station Hotel, was a member of the Church of England and the other best clubs, had thought, during the war, that conscientious objectors were dirty skunks who ought to be shot, thought now that war was damned stupid, was of the opinion that High Churchmen, intellectual novelists, homosexualists, and people who didn't like rugby ought to be kicked out of the country, and that it was a waste of time to learn French, Italian, or German when all the waiters in the best foreign hotels could speak English. As he sat there, manly and ox-like, one felt certain that he would never experience any inclination to revise eucharistic formulae or to rape girls of under sixteen. No; he was the normal healthy man about whom Anglican bishops enthuse when they talk about grit to junior officer cadet corps.

"Oh, Bimmy's not such a bad sort," he drawled, still picking at his moustache. "And it'll be amusing to hear about his miracle."

"*Bimmy!* I thought his name was Jimmy."

"So it is, old girl. So it is. But as his face happens to look rather like his backside... Rather good, don't you think?"

"Sometimes, Alastair, I think that you men are too vulgar for words." Nora Succoth's mind was by no means as emancipated as her legs. "And all I can say is that I'm jolly glad that his rotten dance hall was spirited away to the Bass Rock. And as for his wife, she's as common as you make them. Always winking and rolling her eyes at men when her husband isn't looking."

"Oh, well, if all that one hears is true, Bimmy does a good deal of that sort of thing on his own account."

"And," Nora Succoth went on, "a miracle is just the sort of thing that *would* happen to people like that. A miracle indeed. Did you ever hear of anybody who was at all decent allowing themselves to get mixed up in a miracle? Alastair, if anything like that were to happen to us I'd make you sell out and we'd go and live abroad. But, of course, people like that have no sense of shame. I expect, if you could get at the truth of the matter, you'd find out that they were actually enjoying the publicity."

"I expect they do."

"Alastair." Nora Succoth was leaning forward with her glass in her hand and was regarding her husband with a definitely serious expression on her face. "Alastair. What do *you* make of all this Garden of Eden business?"

Alastair Succoth picked at his moustache with one hand and waved his glass with the other.

"Blest if I know, old girl, blest if I know."

But Nora Succoth continued to look like a youthful Lady Diana Manners hungering for the manna which is from above.

"Yes," she said, "but supposing it's really true? Alastair? Religion and—and Christ and all that?"

Alastair Succoth appeared as unhappy as his general expressionlessness would allow. Like most men to whom the Name of their Saviour is an expletive rather than a noun, he considered that the discussion of religion was at all times the worst of bad form. Golf, wireless, hunting, shooting, these were the things that men could talk about with profit to themselves and to others. But religion! And who would ever have thought that a sensible girl like Nora would get onto that tack. Well, it showed you how careful you had to be of those priests and parsons.

"Look here, Nora," he said, "you're letting this business get on your nerves." He pointed to where the Cinzano and the gin stood side by side. "I'd have another little drink if I were you. It'll do you good."

"But I'm serious, Alastair. Dead serious." And indeed Nora Succoth was looking like a young girl in love with and listening to a poet. "What's your opinion of Christ, Alastair?"

"Oh, I don't know." This time Alastair Succoth felt that he had to give her some kind of answer. "Decent enough sort of fellow, I suppose, but not exactly my line." He reached out and pushed the Cinzano and the gin towards his wife. "Now do have another little drink, old girl. It'll do you good, I tell you."

Nora Succoth sighed, gave up the manna from above, and had another little drink.

3.

THE Shyman Bells arrived in a taxi.

"How are you, my dear?" said Nora Succoth to Mrs. Shyman Bell. "We really must apologize to both of you for bringing you out on a night like this."

"But how silly of you." Bella Shyman Bell was all dimples and good will. "Why, we'd have walked through miles of mud just to have the pleasure of seeing you. Wouldn't we, Jimmy?"

"Of course we would." Mr. J. Shyman Bell was half bending over Mrs. Succoth's hand, like a prudent curate compromising between a bow and a genuflection. "Through miles of mud, Alastair, old boy. For to be perfectly frank, it's not every day of one's life that one has the opportunity of dining with an old pal like you."

After Mrs. Shyman Bell and Alastair Succoth had greeted each other in the same spirit of brassiness a silence fell over the company and, falling, seemed to suggest that those present were not such very great friends after all.

"What about a little spot?" Alastair Succoth asked brightly, just as though hundreds of thousands of other Alastair Succoths in the British Empire were not simultaneously extending the same invitation in the same terms.

Bella Shyman Bell smiled a wide smile which relieved her of the necessity of acquiescing verbally while her husband gave an informed chuckle and said:

"That's the stuff, Alastair. Another little drink, eh? Well, well, where would we all be without it?"

"That's a fact," said Alastair Succoth, busying himself with the bottles.

"What a ducky little dog," said Mrs. Shyman Bell, noticing a small Aberdeen terrier lying curled up on the hearth rug. "Tzoop, tzoop, tzoop." She made sucking noises with her lips. "Snoodger, come here."

But Snoodger merely opened a bored eye, closed it again, and lay still.

"I'm afraid that he's not very sociable." Nora Succoth prodded the dog with her foot. "Get up, Mac, and say 'How-d'ye-do' to the visitors."

"We've got a dog," Bella Shyman Bell informed as she reached out to receive her cocktail from her host. "Billy, we call him. He's a cocker spaniel and such a darling."

"I adore dogs," said Nora Succoth solemnly and as though she were a martyr about to be burnt for her faith. "They're so much more intelligent than cats, don't you think?"

"Well," said Alastair Succoth, holding up his glass, "cheerio, everybody."

Everybody dutifully repeated the salutation and Mrs. Shyman Bell, after a sip at the amber liquid, said sociably:

"Yes, I quite agree with you. Dogs are ever so much more intelligent than cats."

Another silence fell on the company. Mr. Shyman Bell, who always left the main burden of polite conversation to others, began to wonder what his hostess must look like without any clothes on; Nora Succoth thought that Mr. J. Shyman Bell looked uncommonly like a cabman; Bella Shyman Bell asked herself if Nora Succoth's frock was as expensive as it looked; and Alastair Succoth hoped that his guests would leave before eleven.

Nora Succoth was the first to perceive the silence and, realizing that a barrier of noise was the only possible screen between their souls, said at random to Bella Shyman Bell:

"And, my dear, of course we sympathize most frightfully with you about this terrible miracle. And not only us. Everybody's most frightfully sorry for you both. Most frightfully sorry."

Bella Shyman Bell, startled by the unexpected switch from dogs to miracles, made a stiff little inclination with her head.

"I can only assure you," she said, "I can only assure you that both my husband and myself are more than grateful to you for your kind expression of sympathy."

"Yes," said Alastair Succoth. "All that I can say is that it's a damned shame. A damned shame, that's what it is."

"Oh, well," said Mr. Shyman Bell, "we've all got our little crosses to bear, what?"

"A pretty big cross, I should call it." Nora Succoth's third cocktail was beginning to make her feel what she expressed. "If some meddling old priest were to start moving any of *my* belongings I'm afraid that *I* shouldn't be so good-tempered about it."

"Oh, well," said Mr. Shyman Bell, "one must make allowances. These priests aren't as well educated as we are, you know."

"But," protested Alastair Succoth, "you must have dropped a pretty penny over this business, haven't you?"

Mr. J. Shyman Bell folded his hands over his paunch and addressed the fireplace.

"A pretty penny, as you say, old man, and like the other fellow I'm not in business for the good of my health. And the first thing that I did when I got back from North Berwick was to go and see this priest."

"Of course," exclaimed Nora Succoth, "you were in the Garden of Eden when it did a bunk, weren't you? I had quite forgotten that. It must have been too terribly thrilling for words. Weren't you frightened? I know I should have been."

Mr. J. Shyman Bell smiled modestly to the burning coal, to the tongs, and to the bright brass fender.

"I will admit, Mrs. Alastair Succoth, that I was a little bit startled to find myself and my dance hall on the Bass Rock; but the curious part of the affair is that nobody can remember feeling any particular sensation when the building was supposed to be flying through the air. Extraordinary, what?" His hand left his paunch, scratched at his face, went back again. "Well, as I was saying, I went to see this priest and I put it pretty plain and straight to him that I was a stout Protestant and that I couldn't, in loyalty to my forefathers and respect for all that I held most dear, that I couldn't believe in all this mumbo-jumbo and hanky-panky. I said that I was a plain man who was accustomed to dealing with plain facts and I pointed out that, priest or no priest, he had no right to play hide-the-thimble with my dance hall. I said that I didn't give a tinker's curse by what—by what underhand, dago-ish trickery he had removed my property and that either he or the Pope of Rome would have to bring it back right on the dot or pay me cash down a tidy little sum in compensation." He turned to his wife who was three inches taller than he. "Yes, little woman," he said, "I think that, as our American friends would say, J. Shyman showed those illiterate bums just where they got *off*."

"And quite right, too," Alastair Succoth applauded. "That'll teach the swine not to go practising their dirty work on honest, good-living citizens."

"But," asked Nora Succoth, "how *did* the Garden of Eden get onto the Bass Rock? After all, it must have got there somehow."

Mr. J. Shyman Bell made a gesture which he had learned from a lady at Dieppe.

"Mrs. Alastair Succoth," he said, "I'm not a religious man; but I believe in doing good to my fellow-men and in being a true pal in the hour of need. And I think that you may take it from me that this removal of my dance hall is nothing but rank dishonesty and superstition."

"That's right," said Alastair Succoth, afraid that his wife was again going to ask embarrassing questions. "The thing's nothing more nor less than a clever fraud from start to finish. A *clever* fraud, I admit; but nonetheless a fraud for all that."

Nora Succoth nodded.

"I was only wondering," she said apologetically.

Downstairs the gong rumbled, like a giant gripe in a giant belly.

4.

"WHAT I always say," said Alastair Succoth as he passed the port to his guest, "what I always say, Bimmy, is that it's the fellow who knows how to play the game who wins in the long run. Fair play, that's always been my motto and I think, if I may say so without boasting, that it's a very British motto. For, when all is said and done, it's fair play that has won Britain her place among the nations. What I always say is that the world is divided into two classes: Britishers and wops, white men and yellow men. What say you, Bimmy?"

The ladies had left the room two minutes previously and the men were now free to indulge in manly man-to-man conversation.

"You've hit the nail on the head, Alastair, old man." Mr. J. Shyman Bell's mind was at a loss to know whether it was misted more by the alcohol which had come or by that which was yet to come. "Being British, that's what matters." He raised his hand to his mouth, but too late, for a large hiccup had already escaped and was now sailing magnificently round the room. " 'Scuse me, Alastair old boy; but your wines are so good that I can't help belching out of sheer appreciation. Yes, and sometimes I say to myself in the still watches of the night: 'Bimmy, old lad, if you suddenly woke up to find that you weren't British you'd shoot yourself.' "

"British. Yes, Bimmy, we're British." Mr. Alastair Succoth pronounced the *Cives Romani Sumus* as though it were the first article of the Nicaean Creed. "And that's more than priests and miracle-mongers can say, Bimmy. No person who was really and truly and wholly British would pinch another fellow's dance hall and wheich it away to the top of the Bass Rock."

Mr. J. Shyman Bell gulped at his port.

"Alastair, old scout," he said, "I can see that you're a man after my own heart. It's a funny thing, but one doesn't run into such a hell of a lot of people who think the same thing as we do: about being British and all that. And you're quite right about the miracle. It was one of the most un-British things that I've seen in all my life."

"Yes, Bimmy, and you can take my word for it that it won't stop there. You won't get a penny compensation, not a penny. It doesn't matter what the priest said to you. I know their tricks. All he's got to do is to wire to the Pope and ask for an indulgence to do the dirty on a stout Protestant. Oh, yes, I know their tricks. They're not trained in those seminatories or whatever they call them for nothing. No, Bimmy, my boy, you'll be lucky if you see a brass farthing."

Mr. J. Shyman Bell protested through his round, red balloon of a face.

"But, damn it, Alastair, the fellow promised."

"Promised!" Alastair gave a Muirfield washing-room laugh. "Promised! Damn it, Bimmy, those fellows don't think anything of promises. The end justifies the means, as the Jesuists say. And these Jesuists are all over the country, lighting candles and burning incense and plotting and planning to ruin our womenfolk and to make a Roman Catholic lord provost of Edinburgh. Jesuists. I'll bet this priest is a Jesuist in disguise. If he isn't one himself, his father was." He blew out a cloud of smoke, deliberately, self-consciously, as though the act were an accomplishment and symbolic of virility. "But I'll tell you how you can get your own back, Bimmy. You can turn your Garden of Eden into a sort of casino and rake in the shekels. That'll make the cads sit up, Bimmy, that'll make the cads sit up."

"A casino?" Mr. J. Shyman Bell's sense of acquisitiveness (described by him as a business brain) had been somewhat dulled by wine. "A casino, Alastair? But why a casino?"

"To show those rotters the true meaning of British pluck, Bimmy.

And, as I say, you'd fairly coin money. Far more than you did when the Garden of Eden was in Edinburgh. Damn it, man, North Berwick's becoming more and more fashionable every year. Golf, of course. But, apart from the hotels, there's no first-class dancing place where people can go in the evening. And they'd be only too glad to take a launch out to the Bass Rock after dinner and shake a hoof and have a drink or two. The miracle may be a hoax, Bimmy, but that's no reason why you shouldn't use the hoax to your own advantage. The Garden of Eden's famous all over the world now. You'd get Americans coming all the way from Ohio to dance on the Bass Rock. People'd be tickled to death at the thought of being able to dance in the original Garden of Eden stuck on top of the Bass Rock by the treachery of a priest. Damn it, man, the place is still yours. All you'd have to do to make it really international would be to get a special license to sell drink till all hours and provide some ootchy-looking actressy sort of girls to sit alone under palms. And you'd make money hand over fist."

"Alastair, you're a pal." Mr. J. Shyman Bell's soul was glowing almost as redly as his face. Already he could see the purple and red and gold lights shining out across the water from the Bass Rock. Already he could see the launches filled with well-dressed and well-fed men and women putting out from the harbour. Already he could see himself receiving them at the top of the carpeted steps. He'd open in ten days' time while the miracle was still hot. On Christmas night for preference. Lots of people would motor down from Edinburgh. From Glasgow even. From Dundee. From Perth. From Aberdeen. He'd see that priest tomorrow and tell him he could put his hundred thousand pounds where the monkey put the nuts. Yes, Alastair was indeed a pal.

"Not at all," Alastair Succoth protested as Mr. J. Shyman Bell thanked him for the seventh time. "Not at all, Bimmy. After all, it's only British to help a friend."

"British. Yes, it's a great thing to be British." Mr. J. Shyman Bell's sense of acquisitiveness dulled again into hoggish content. "By the way, Alastair," he asked, leaning across the table and speaking through the fingers of his right hand, "by the way, Alastair, did I ever tell you that one about the newly married couple in the railway carriage?"

CHAPTER X

1.

SATURDAY, the seventeenth of December, was the octave of the miracle; and, as though to celebrate the fact, the more shrieking of the great dailies published summaries of all the opinions expressed thereon by prominent people during the week. The most metropolitan of deans came, of course, an easy first with a hundred or so public condemnations of magic masquerading as religion and of an outworn sophistry, credited only by Irishmen and Spaniards, which was making a last grotesque struggle to justify itself in the eyes of thinking men. A very eminent female writer on contraceptives was also quoted as stating that the miracle was just "one more instance of latent Freudianism becoming patent," though how she had arrived at this conclusion was not reported. *Punch* was represented by two hearty cartoons: one of the goalkeeper of a much-pressed association football team beseeching the shade of Father Malachy to translate his goal a few hundred yards farther down the field; and another of a drunken reveller prodding to find the keyhole of his front door and blaming Father Malachy for having stolen it. The *Church Times*, that gentleman in a chasuble and a top hat, had written: "While remaining perfectly open to conviction of the supernatural character of the recent extraordinary happenings by the Firth of Forth, we would state quite clearly that, even if the alleged miracle turns out to have been an actual miracle, we cannot accept these events, however remarkable in themselves, as constituting in any way a definite proof of the Petrine claims; and we would remind our readers that miracles are not the especial prerogative of the Roman Church as is instanced by the little-known fact that one of the early Oxford Tractarians, within the memory of the writer's grandfather, once caused a decapitated frog to become alive again by invoking the aid of Saint Charles the First." The *Tablet,* the glory of English Romanism, did not gulp the miracle any more gluttonishly than its Anglican contemporary but stated that, while miracles were, and had always been, possible, it would be as well to await the expression of competent hierarchical opinion; and the *Universe,* the *Daily Mail* of the Faith, had come out with photographs of the Bass Rock and of the bishop of Midlothian pontificating the *Te Deum* in front of the quondam site of the Garden of Eden but, like its more sedate aunt, had cautioned: "Don't believe until you have to." The Brighton *Baptist* and the Liverpool *Eugenist* had been equally vituperative.

But, as the shrieking dailies informed their millions, the hit of the week had been the verse sung at Newcastle by the leading lady of the *Whose Baby Are You?* company:

"*Malachy, your mericle,*
Has made us all hysterical.
For we had to fly
Right through the sky
Until we reached North Berwickle."

Father Malachy saddened as he read these summaries. The thing was so evidently of God, and yet even those of the household of the Faith were cautious about accepting it as such. What hope was there for a world which insisted on preferring Barabbas to Christ, Barabbas with a saxophone, Barabbas with a wireless set, Barabbas with his ladies who thought it intellectual to be light, Barabbas who couldn't believe in God because he believed so much in himself?

Tears gathered in his eyes as he gazed, mentally, out over the world. Everywhere faith seemed to be dying, in Andalucía as in Clackmannan, in Brittany as in Los Angeles. And Scotland, bonnie, darling Scotland which had always cared for the things of God, bonnie, darling Scotland was going the same way as France and South America. No God, no worship, no true love; just investment companies and cinemas and hotel lounges. Oh, for the days when there was a mitred abbot at Dunfermline and a cardinal archbishop of St. Andrews who rode in scarlet and ermine. Oh, for the days when faith was faith and love was love and the altar was the trysting place of heaven and earth. Oh, for the days when the incense rose in Melrose and the sacring bell was heard in Jedburgh. Oh, for the days when the Church of God was the Church of God in gold and silver for all men to see and not a despised remnant slouching along back streets in ungainly coats and bagging trousers.

And yet they could come again, those dead days. They could come again, like flowers after a long winter. They could come again, John Henry Newman's Second Spring in Scotland. They could come again, those days when St. Andrews should ring as Sevilla and Dunkeld as Bologna, those days when the Blessed Sacrament should be carried again through the tired streets and men and women would know It for God-with-us. Yes, they would come again if men would only humble themselves and believe, they could come again, those days when Scotland was Scotland and not just a strident suburb of New York.

His eyes dried as his heart cheered and he got up and moved to the window. Yes, there was a crowd outside the site of the miracle. Some kneeling, some gaping, some looking as though they didn't know whether to gape or to kneel. No, no, all was not yet lost.

Lourdes didn't get itself believed in in a day. His miracle might yet convert the world.

Reassured, he was about to turn back when a sudden burst of song crashed itself upon his ears:

> "*Malachy, your mericle,*
> *Has made us all hysterical.*
> *For we had to fly*
> *Right through the sky*
> *Until we reached North Berwickle.*"

A band of urchins, probably. He didn't want to see. The tears came again, streaming this time. "O Blessed Jesus," he prayed, "make them see, make them see. Bring the world back, bring Scotland back; be met on the road to Rannoch as You were once met on the road to Emmaus." And the tears went on streaming, spreading out into tributaries as they flowed.

2.

BUT he dried his tears quickly enough when James shouted through the locked door that that fat man with the Johnnie Walker face was waiting in the parlour to see him.

He found Mr. J. Shyman Bell wearing the expression which the latter considered to be appropriate to a stout Protestant about to converse with a devout Roman Catholic.

"Good morning, Father Malachy Murdoch," said his visitor, who was looking very natty in what his tailors had described as an autumn grey suiting.

Father Malachy bowed. Poor Scotland, he was thinking. Up on Princes Street slim, silk legs were passing, slim, silk legs which were neither for Him nor against Him.

"I think," began Mr. J. Shyman Bell when they were both seated,

"I think that the object of my visit will not entirely displease you. On the contrary, Father Malachy Murdoch, on the contrary. For I have come to tell you that I intend to waive all claim to damages for the losses I have suffered in respect of your very religious miracle."

"But that is most generous of you." Father Malachy's heart began to go out to the other, in spite of his somewhat this-worldly appearance. Perhaps God had touched his heart. Perhaps he was going to ask to be received into the Church. Saint Augustine had been a Shyman Bell before Grace touched him. "And may I ask what has made you change your mind?"

The stout Protestant scratched at his face.

"The fact is," he said, "I've suddenly realized that the Garden of Eden is all right where it is. Very much all right. You see, North Berwick is a fashionable place and people have no decent place to dance in. Why shouldn't they dance on the Bass Rock, Father Malachy Murdoch? Eh, why shouldn't they? Romantic situation, nice little sail after dinner. A novelty, in fact. And what interests people these days is novelty. All that's wanted is a first-class London band and the concern will go like hot cakes. And I think, Father Malachy Murdoch, that it's an excellent way out of a rather difficult situation. You'll have brought off your religious miracle and I'll continue to make money out of my dance hall and we'll both be happy, what?"

"Mr. Shyman Bell, I'd very much prefer that you let the old arrangement stand." Father Malachy's voice was even and strong with the strength of a river swinging to the sea. "Only yesterday I all but concluded an arrangement which should provide me with sufficient money to compensate both your friend Mr. Bleater and yourself. Some financial details, it is true, remain in suspense for the time being; but I do not think that there is any doubt about the financial success of my venture."

What had the fellow been up to? Mr. Shyman Bell wondered. Exporting pretty nuns to Buenos Aires, probably. These priests knew all the dodges.

"I don't want the money," he said. "I want the Garden of Eden to remain where it is. In the middle of the sad sea waves." He laughed the skeleton of a laugh. "And you can give your hundred thousand pounds to some deserving charity."

Father Malachy thought. This was terrible. The ultimate blasphemy. But perhaps Mr. Ink would be willing to give him two hundred thousand, one hundred and thirteen pounds, nineteen shillings. Perhaps if he were to put in a couple of extra lectures, say, in Bristol and Dundee...

"If I were to make it two hundred thousand, Mr. Shyman Bell, would that make you reconsider your decision?"

Mr. Shyman Bell started. Two hundred thousand pounds. Yes, it must be nuns. Probably pretty convent girls of under fifteen as well. But that wasn't his affair. And two hundred thousand pounds was certainly a large sum of money. A very large sum of money.

"I would have to have a guarantee," he said. "A guarantee. Now and in writing."

Father Malachy shook his head mournfully.

"Before I could do that, Mr. Shyman Bell, I'd have to ask you to give me time to make further arrangements."

About the convent girls, no doubt. Get the bishop's permission, perhaps. And the bishop might be frightened in case it leaked out. No, old Alastair was right. He had said that he wouldn't see a penny of his money. All *mañana,* this sort of stuff. Alastair was a stockbroker and knew what he was talking about. He had as much chance of getting two hundred thousand pounds as he had of getting two hundred bawbees. And the Garden of Eden, world-famous on top of the Bass Rock, might easily bring in half a million.

"No," he declined aloud, "not for any money you like to offer me, Father Malachy Murdoch. The Garden of Eden on the Bass Rock is likely to turn out a very sound commercial proposition and, while preserving every respect for your feelings in the matter, I intend to exploit it for what it is worth. I am going down to North Berwick this afternoon to make arrangements about a license with the local authorities; and I intend to open the new Garden of Eden on Christmas night."

It was some few minutes before Father Malachy spoke.

"Mr. Shyman Bell," he said slowly, "you have styled yourself a stout Protestant; and, as far as I am aware, stout Protestants have always professed a deep love and reverence for Our Blessed Lord. Because of that and because for the moment I see no other course open to me, I am going to appeal to you in the Sacred Name of Him Whom you worship as your Saviour. The transference of the Garden of Eden to the Bass Rock, Mr. Shyman Bell, was performed by your Saviour and by my Saviour, by your God and by my God, in order that His people should leave off from running after vain things and should turn again to Him with faith and with love. If you continue to use your dance hall which has been so singularly honoured by God, if you continue to use it for its original purposes—and especially to use it on the place in which it is now located—then you will be committing a horrible blasphemy. I am perfectly willing to compensate you up to the extent of two hundred thousand pounds for the losses which you have received, but you must give me time to make my final arrangements for obtaining the money. All that I ask of you at present is to refrain from doing this very horrible thing and I ask you in the name of Almighty God."

Behind the red bladder Mr. Shyman Bell was most thoroughly miserable. It was just like this damned priest to drag religion into an affair which was, when all was said and done, pure business from beginning to end. Oh, yes, they could trot out the soft soap all right, these priests. But he was too cute a bird to be taken that way. By God, he was. And Alastair Succoth would laugh like hell if he allowed himself to be led up the garden by a lot of holy-Jesus-this and holy-Jesus-that.

"Father Malachy Murdoch," he said as convincingly as he could, "there is no man on this earth who has a deeper and more sincere respect for religion than I have. But religion, after all, is a private affair and ought not to obtrude itself into commerce. In other words, business is business, Father Malachy Murdoch, and, while continuing to have my deep and sincere respect for religion, I must abide by my decision to stick to my dance hall."

Father Malachy nodded.

"I see," he said. "I see."

3.

As he was coming away from the door James handed him a telegram which read:

Undertake no public contract until I have consulted Rome.
ALOYSIUS, ABBOT OF FORT WILLIAM

And, as he crumpled the paper in his hands, from without came words which gradually became more and more distinct:

"*. . . quite hysterical.*
For we had to fly
Right through the sky
Until we reached North Berwickle."

Poor Father Malachy; it was his dark hour.

CHAPTER XI

1.

THE Right Reverend Monsignor Robert Gillespie, lord bishop of Midlothian, was sitting in his dull study with his spectacles half down his nose and his breviary half off his lap. On the green walls around him Saint Teresa wallowed in God and Saint Francis of Assisi preached to the birds and the cardinal archbishop of Venta de Baños handed a bag of liquorice balls to Jackie Coogan and groups of Bearsden seminarians looked stoutly and ruggedly out upon the Caledonia which they hoped to conquer.

His lordship was feeling content. He had had a kipper for his tea and a wee bit blether with Monsignor McOgle from Gorebridge. It was a pity, though, that he had still so much office to say. "*Dixit Dominus Domino meo...*" he murmured unenthusiastically and stopped. Aye-he. If only yon Malachy would invent some way in which bishops could say their office without saying it, if he'd only do that now it'd be as good as flitting a hundred paly de donces. "*...donec ponam inimicos tuos scabellum pedum tuorum.*" Aye, if there were only a bit more *scabellum pedum* about this miracle it wouldn't be a bad thing. But thae heretics didn't seem to be keen on becoming anybody's footstool, not they. They were taking the miracle just as though it were a military tattoo at Dreghorn. Only this afternoon when he had been pontificating the *Te Deum* he had seen a lassie sucking jujubes. And all thae ministers and novelists and loose actresses saying that the miracle was all fiddlesticks. Och, well, God would give them fiddlesticks in the long run. He would that. "*Gloria Patri, et Filio, et Spiritui Sancto; . . . sæculasaeculorumamen.*" Well, there was another psalm finished. Aye, aye, what with yon Malachy and yon female schismatics in short skirts a bishop's life was worse than a pleeceman's, so it was. "*. . . saeculasæculorumamen.*" Bang went another yin. He'd soon be at the *Magnificat* at this rate.

But at the *Magnificat* he boggled. "*Quia respexit,*" he bumbled and re-bumbled. "*Quia respexit humilitatem ancillae suae,*" he got out and yawned. Och, well, it was no use going on if he felt like this. He'd have a wee read to himself. Just a page or two.

"'The plans,'" he read in the book which he had substituted for his breviary,

> "the plans are hidden in the factory to which, surrounded as it is by spies on all sides, it is most difficult to gain access." "Bah," she cried, stamping her Rue-de-la-Paix-shod foot, "yellow blood courses through your veins, Sir Richard, or you would not abandon to ruin and dishonour the granddaughter of the woman who bore both our fathers." "Cynthia," he pleaded, clenching his fists until the nails bit deep into the flesh . . .

In five minutes the book slid to the floor and the lord bishop of Midlothian, successor of Kentigern, Ninian, and Columba, was asleep.

2.

But he did not sleep for long for Jeannie, the episcopal *bonne à tout faire,* popped her trollop head round the door and said:

"Ma lurrd, there's a preest wi' a bit reed uner his collar wants tae see ye."

"What?" asked the bishop, who had been dreaming about plans being hidden under the Bass Rock. "What did you say, Jeannie?"

Jeannie repeated:

"Ma lurrd, there's a preest wi' a bit reed uner his collar wants tae see ye."

"A bit reed, is there?" The bishop, like all forty-winkers, was not in the best of tempers at being awakened. "A bit *red,* Ah suppose ye mean. How often have Ah told ye to learn to speak English?"

Jeannie curtsied.

"Ah beg yer parrdon, ma lurrd," she said.

"That's funny, though." The bishop was thinking aloud. "It must be a cardinal; but there are no cardinals gallivanting round Edinburgh as far as Ah'm aware. What does he look like, Jeannie?"

Jeannie spoke in a low voice.

"Awfy slinky and mysteerious and forrun," she said.

"Och, well, tell him to come ben."

"*Buona sera, Monsignore,*" said the preest wi' the bit reed uner his collar when he came ben. "*Io sono il Cardinale Vassena di Santa Maria della Pace e sono stato delegato dalla Sua Santità per verificare are il suo piccolo miracolo scozzese.*"

"Eh?" said the bishop. "What's that ye said?"

The newcomer smiled.

"*Non parla italiano? E il francese? Senza dubbio, sans doute vous parlez le français? Eh bien, commençons encore une fois. Je suis le Cardinal Vassena de Sainte Marie de la Paix et j'ai été délégué par Sa Sainteté pour vérifer votre petit miracle écossais.*"

But the bishop continued to shake his head.

"In that case," said the newcomer in clipped but idiomatic

English, "we shall have to speak English. Let us commence again. I am Cardinal Vassena of Saint Mary of the Peace and I have been delegated by His Hol-i-ness to verify your little Scotsz mirackil."

The bishop was about to sink on one knee, but the cardinal prevented him with a gesture.

"No," he said. "We are both bee-shops together, if you know what I mean, and I think that we can dispense with these little po-lite-nesses."

The bishop pointed to the chair in which he had just been dozing.

"Sit ye down, yer eminence," he said. "Ah'm sorry that Ah've just finished ma tea, but Jeannie could heat ye up something in no time."

His eminence shook his head.

"Tea and theology never blend," he said. "Still less do viskee and theology blend if one may judge by the state of religion in your country."

"Aye," said the bishop, "Scotland's got the releegious measles all right. What wi' ceenimas and congregationalists, we're in pretty much the same state as Rome under Neero. Well, well, yer eminence, they canna say Ah havna warned them. Ah've preached on Calvinism and immoral nightdresses till Ah was blue in the face. But it doesna seem to do much good; Jenners† and the General Assembly are always with us."

"Well," said the cardinal, who had not completely understood the bishop's topical allusion, "it certainly seems as though you had been letting off the fireworks lately. Cabarets that fly through the air like aëroplanes. *Per Bacco,* but it is much more spectacular than anything that has happened in Italy for centuries."

"Ah didna see it maself," said the bishop. "But they do say that it was as good as the fleeing House of Loretto any day of the week."

The cardinal's face darkened.

"*Questo Padre...* this Father Malachy? What sort of a priest is

† The Maison Worth of Edinburgh.

he?"

"Malachy? Och, he's a braw, bricht laddie all right. A bit ower-impatient for the Kingdom o' God among us, but a braw, bricht laddie for all that."

The cardinal was as perplexed by the braw, bricht laddie as the bishop had been by *il suo piccolo miracolo scozzese.*

"I beg your pardon," he said, "but I am afraid that I have not fully understood."

"Malachy's all right," the bishop anglicized. "All have nothing but good words for him. Canon Geoghegan got a len' o' him from the abbot of Fort William to put his curates through their liturgical paces and Ah must say that what he doesn't know about *Ite Missa est* and all yon could be written on the back o' a Children o' Mary meedal. And the canon's mighty pleased at the flitting o' the dancing hall from his parish as it appears there was all sorts o' hanky-panky going on."

The cardinal translated aloud for his own benefit.

"*Credo che capisco.* Father Malachy did not entirely confine himself to his liturgical duties, but went so far as morally to cleanse the parish by removing a cabaret that was a little worldly."

"*Verra* worldly," said the Bishop. "Carryings on at both the afternoon and evening sessions. Ah ken all about it; the canon tellt me."

"But," persisted the cardinal, "I gather that that was not his official reason for removing this cabaret *un poco mondano.* And, indeed, if ecclesiastics were to make a habit of removing cabarets every time that they exceeded the theological definition of chastity, well, Monsignore, I am afraid that the air would be filled with flying cabarets. Even in Rome itself there are establishments which I should imagine are much more subversive of morality than anything which you possess in Scotland. But that, I suppose, is a question of climate rather than of ecclesiastical discipline. *La giovinezza italiana...*" The cardinal smiled wisely. "No, most certainly a more cogent reason was required; and from the newspapers as well as from my good friend the cardinal archbishop of Westminster I understand that this Benedictine monk took it upon himself to translate the Garden of Eden to the Bass Rock in order to bring people back to faith in our most Illustrious Saviour Jesus Christ."

"Ye've got it," said the bishop. "Malachy had his fill o' unbelief and he wanted to see if he couldna make folks believe for a change."

"I see." The cardinal nodded as though to shake the knowledge well down into his head. "I see. But do you think that a Benedictine monk has any right to take upon himself a task which might have been left safely enough to the Roman authorities?"

"Ah'm no so sure that Ah don't think he has," said the bishop. "It's the business of every priest, be he monk or high heid yin, to save souls from the lusts of the flesh and the perneecious serpent o' heresy."

"Yes," said the cardinal, "but by the ordinary channels: by saying Mass, by hearing confessions, by distributing Holy Communion, by preaching. Monsignore, I will be frank with you. This Scotsz mirackil of yours is not liked in Rome. Propaganda is against it; the Sacred Congregation of Rites is against it; the Holy Father himself is against it. You see, the prevalent opinion is that the time is not yet ripe for such very spectacular evidences of the truth of our religion. In Italy last year fifty-seven statues of the Most Holy Madonna were reputed to have wept and there were at least fourteen cases of alleged stigmata. In Spain there were three appearances of the Blessed Virgin and in the Valdepinones a cock was stated to have laid a golden egg on the high altar of the parish church."

"That's as may be," said the bishop, "but a cock laying a golden egg on the high altar of the parish church of Valdy-Thingummy is no the same as flitting a paly de donce from Auld Reeky to the Bass Rock."

"We do not deny," the cardinal sailed on, "we do not deny that these things *may* be the work of Divine Providence; but it is equally possible that they may be the work of an as yet unknown material law or of the Devil or of a minor Celtic saint with not enough to occupy his time in the heavenly courts. And as they are not *manifestly* of Divine Providence we feel that it would be imprudent officially or unofficially to recognize them as mirackils. The world is ever ready to mock at the Catholic Church, Monsignore; and these mirackils to prove mirackils generally finish by bringing further disrespect upon that which they seek to establish. You must admit that the reception of your Scotsz mirackil by the public press of all countries has been preponderantly hostile and that sacred things have thereby been held up to the ridicule of the ignorant and uninstructed masses. Monsignore, you are a bee-shop of the Catholic Church; and I do not think that I ought to require to tell you that it has always been the policy of Rome to verify every matter before making a definite pronouncement upon it. We are the guardians of truth, Monsignore, and we cannot afford to act hastily. The Immaculate Conception had to wait eighteen hundred and fifty-four years before it was defined as an article of faith; and, in view of that fact and of the policy which it represents, I am afraid, Monsignore, that the authorities will take a very serious view of your authorizing and yourself pontificating six consecutive solemn *Te Deums* on the site of the alleged mirackil."

"Ah didna do it without conseederable reflection," said the bishop. "And if ye don't believe me ye can ask Malachy himself. Ah was dead against the miracle until ma own scallywag of a brother came and told me that he had been in the Garden of Eden when it fleed awa' and that he didna believe a wurrd of it. When Aundry told me yon Ah was persuaded that the miracle was a wurrk o' God; and, with all due respect to yer eminence, Ah think that if yer eminence had had Aundry for a brother yer eminence would have been persuaded just as Ah was."

"Monsignore," said the cardinal kindly, "I quite understand your point of view. You are bee-shop of a diocese in which what is apparently a mirackil has occurred. You wish, naturally, to honour God for honouring you. You sing *Te Deums* and you prostrate yourself. *Si, si, Monsignore, comprendo perfettamente. Perfettamente, Monsignore. Ma*... but I must ask you to look at the happening as it is related to the Catholic Church throughout the world, to the Catholic Church in France, in Spain, in Germany, in Italy, in Poland, in Australia. At the present moment, Monsignore, we must not estrange people from essentials by insisting on unessentials; we have enough to do to get people to swallow the necessary mirackils without trying to pour down a few extra ones. The Incarnation, the Resurrection, the Presence of Our Lord in the Blessed Sacrament, these are the things to insist on. And then once we have been granted these"—the cardinal smiled—"once we have been granted these, Monsignore, we may begin to think about cocks which lay golden eggs on high altars and cabarets which fly through the air. But for the moment we must take care not to sacrifice the sacred certainties to the potentially sacred possibilities."

"Aye," said the bishop, "but it was precisely to bring folks back to thae sacred certainties that Malachy flitted yon paly de donce."

The cardinal inclined his head.

"So you have already explained; and I have already pointed out that these wonders to prove wonders work more harm than good. Look at the press of your own country. Listen to the echoes of the blasphemies that have been uttered because of your reported mirackil. Believe me, Monsignore, it was not for nothing that the Holy Father sent me to Edinburgh; he did not send me to Valdepinones."

The bishop nodded lugubriously.

"Aye," he said, "aye."

"And," continued the cardinal, "I think that I may claim to have been fair. I have been among you for three days now and I have both seen for myself and see as others see; and, before leaving for Rome tonight, I thought it only courteous to call upon you and inform you of the recommendations which I intend to make to the Holy Father."

The bishop nodded still more lugubriously.

"Aye," he said. "Ye'll be telling His Holiness that we're a lot of auld sweetie wives and His Holiness will close down our miracle." He snuffled away to himself. "Och, well, Ah suppose ye canna have it both ways; sporrans and the supernatural never did agree. But ye can tell His Holiness from me—with all due respect, mind ye—ye can tell His Holiness that we're a hard-heided lot in Scotland and that when we have miracles we have miracles and not just a lot o' daft cocks laying eggs on altars."

"Perhaps," said the cardinal, "you would prefer to convey the message personally on the occasion of your next visit *ad limina apostolorum.*"

"Och," said the bishop, scratching his ear, "dinna fash yerself, yer eminence. No harm meant. Ah was just having ma wee bit gurn to maself. But it's no use greetin' ower spilt milk and Ah suppose it's still less use greetin' ower spiled miracles. The Lorrd giveth and the Lorrd taketh away. Blessed be the Name o' the Lorrd."

"Yes," said the cardinal. "And it's not as if the mirackil were condemned. Far from it. In the fullness of time, Monsignore, it may well be that Almighty God will give us a definite confirmation that your mirackil is a true mirackil. In the fullness of time, Monsignore. But until then no more solemn *Te Deums,* no more public services. Private devotions, if you will, but nothing to arouse criticism or retard the cause of Christ."

"Aye," said the bishop in much the same tone as, when a small boy, he had used to the village schoolmaster.

They dined together, the cardinal and the bishop, and talked the holy shop of prelates while in the dark Church of Saint Margaret of Scotland Father Malachy prayed for strength to endure and to conquer and in Newcastle a fair-haired girl of twenty-one, in clothes that were the fashion in italics, waggled her free-thinking little posterior and sang that they had had to fly right through the sky until they reached North Berwickle.

CHAPTER XII

1.

"*ET puis*," Mr. J. Shyman Bell was explaining in his astoundingly flawless French to three of the ootchy-looking actressy sort of girls for whom he had telegraphed to Paris, "*et puis vous vous mettrez dans les petits coins, n'est-ce pas? tout-à-fait comme si vous étiez au Rat Mort. Et si le bonheur veut qu'un bel agent de bourse se mette avec vous, tant mieux pour vous et tant mieux pour la maison. Mais pas de galanteries sur place, hein? Après, si vous voulez: dans une chambre d'hôtel, sur la plage même, sur le golf course si ça vous fait envie. Alors, c'est entendu comme ça?*"

The three girls smiled among themselves. They were pretty, frivolous and had chosen their profession as much as it had chosen them.

"*Oui, monsieur le patron*," assured a small girl with auburn hair, roving pale blue eyes and a slim body which looked as though it had been poured into her frock. "*Oui, monsieur le patron, nous comprenons parfaitement. D'ailleurs dans toutes les meilleures boites de nuit montmartroises il faut toujours se tenir comme à la messe.*"

"*C'est cela, Yvette. Comme à la messe. Et après.*" Mr. J. Shyman Bell scratched his scar and made an exterior boulevard gesture. "*Après, mes petites chattes, débrouillez-vous; c'est votre affaire et Papa Jimmy s'en fiche pas mal.*"

Yes, he thought, as he walked away on a final tour of inspection, a Garden of Eden on the Bass Rock was worth two in the street. One thousand tickets at thirty shillings each had been issued and snapped up within twelve hours. Since then some of them had changed hands for as many pounds as they had cost shillings. And tomorrow night the place was booked up and the next and the next again. Americans were already cabling to reserve tables for the Great Good Friday Novelty Night. Yes, he had done well to listen to Alastair and not to allow himself to be bamboozled by that crafty priest.

And what a *première* it was going to be. Deauville, Long Island, or the Lido had never seen anything like it. Talk about up-to-dateness. As the Americans would say, it was right up to God's last minute and then some. To begin with, the whole chorus of the *Whose Baby Are You?* company were going to be present and Miss Gertie de la Muette, the principal girl, was going to pop out of a large mince pie at midnight and sing "Malachy, your miracle." Damned decent of that sporting peer fellow, Lord Stitcham, to have offered to bring them over from Newcastle in his private fleet of monoplanes. Damned decent, but then Stitcham was one of the old brigade and no mistake. Anybody who'd ever seen him at Le Touquet with a bunch of pretty actresses sitting on the bonnet of his Rolls could be pretty certain that miracles would have nothing on Stitcham. And that dean fellow. Of course it was kind of him to have offered to broadcast at eleven forty-five on "There Lives More Faith in Honest Doubt...."; but it was just possible that some of the more skittish Writers to the Signet[†] might find the theme a little highbrow. Still, there had been no refusing the fellow; one couldn't do anything when one came up against a parson who was three times as worldly as oneself. And in any case Miss Gertie de la Muette, who was going to sign and raffle

† *Chic* Edinburgh lawyers.

the silk stockings which she had worn during the flight of the Garden of Eden, would cheer up the lowbrows. Yes, yes, it promised to be a first-class do all right.

He went down to the basement, which was welded into the Bass Rock as though socketed by man and not by God and, after telephoning unnecessarily to Edinburgh, Dunbar, Glasgow, Aberdeen, and Liverpool, had a few wee hoots to himself for the sake of Auld Lang Syne and Mr. J. Shyman Bell.

2.

As early as half-past nine the motor launches began to put out from the shore and to speed, like inspirations flashing through a tired brain, across the rippling dark sea towards the Bass Rock.

Every hotel in North Berwick was filled with guests desirous of assisting at what an assertive popular periodical had described as "the most startling epoch-making thrill of the century." From Edinburgh had come everybody who was anybody: the chartered accountants who were able to live in the West End because they ran their offices on the labour of apprentices to whom they repaid as salary the sums which the apprentices' Fathers had advanced to them as indenture fees; the solicitors, more widely read than the chartered accountants and, when earning more than two thousand a year, Anglican to the last ditch, by Gad; the barristers, called advocates, the most cultured of the lot and disbelieving, as the cultured must do, in all religions from Buddhism to Holy Rollerism; the butchers, the bakers, the candlestick-makers whose shops were large enough not to be noticed; and the wives, as young as they felt, of the chartered accountants, stockbrokers, lawyers, barristers, butchers, bakers, candlestick-makers, and their daughters, with eyes like Icelandic saints and knees like light ladies from Cadiz, and their sons, clean, healthy British lads every man jack of them. Glasgow, too, had Daimlered through her shipbuilders and colliery owners and Dundee had yielded up her jute merchants and Aberdeen and Inverness had sent the more wealthy and internationally minded of their young married sets. From London, too, had come a magnate or two and from New York a divorced Russian princess who had said, as she walked out of her million-dollar home, to her husband and every newspaper in the world: "S'long, Billie boy; come around soon," and who had, so they said, the cutest lil private bar you *ever* saw in her luxurious marble bathroom. And from Paris, to show his faith in the cause of unfaith, had flown a prominent Freemason who earned his living by swallowing live goldfish and spewing them up, still alive, into a pre-Reformation chamber pot. So that the *bon ton* was very much there although everybody regretted that the Aga Khan had been unavoidably prevented from attending.

At half-past nine, then, the launches began to put out and the daughters of Murrayfield and Morningside and Kelvinside and Tennessee, hugging themselves inside their cloaks, told one another that it was cold but, my dear, the experience was just too thrilling for words.

In one of the launches Jean Moorbotham, pretty, twenty-two, and about to be married at the Church of Saint John the Evangelist, turned to her hefty mother whose husband had made a few hundred thousands out of pre-war whisky.

"Mums," she troodled, "why can't *our* clergyman perform a miracle?"

"Eh?" said Mrs. Moorbotham, who had been wondering if the installation of a private cinema on their Perthshire estate would attract guests who had hitherto refused her invitations.

"Why can't *our* clergyman perform a miracle, Mums?" her daughter repeated. "I'm sure he could bring off a pretty nifty one if he tried."

Theology was not Mrs. Moorbotham's strong suit. Still, she did her best.

"Only Roman Catholics believe in miracles, Jean," she reprimanded. "Only uneducated people who are deceived by their deceitful priests into believing that—that they can get their sins forgiven for five shillings and that the Virgin Mary will judge the quick and the dead. A well-read man like dear Canon Ingot would simply never dream of doing any such thing."

"I see," said Jean as she turned once more to look across the water to where the Garden of Eden splashed ruby and gold upon the merging indigo of sky and sea.

In another launch three prominent fornicators conversed together in manly tones.

"Bloody good idea of Bimmy Bell's, rigging this show up like this. And they say that there's no end of booze on the premises." The speaker, a red-headed stockbroker, picked meditatively at the lobe of his ear. "And Archie MacGuff was telling me that Bimmy's laid in a plentiful supply of jaunty Janes. Real hot stuff, you know. None of your Stockbridge blancmanges."

"French tarts," said a solicitor to the Supreme Court. "Well, you can bet your bottom dollar that old Charlie's going to do some parley-voo tonight."

"And," said a cooper from Leith, "they say that the chorus of *Whose Baby Are You?* are going to be there. Me for that little bunch of cuties. I never was any good at getting into bed in French."

"Anyway," said the red-haired stockbroker, "Bimmy's certainly shown the jolly old Pope that Scotland's not standing for any foreign interference."

"He has that," echoed the solicitor to the Supreme Court and the cooper from Leith.

3.

Mr. J. Shyman Bell, all white and pink and shining, stood at the top of the four steps in the vestibule and shook hands personally with every guest.

"Good evening, Mrs. Barton-Smythe. This is indeed a great pleasure. And *Miss* Barton-Smythe. How *very* charming. Ah, Sir James!

This is a great honour, Sir James. Yes, as I said only half an hour ago to the representatives of the press, we are opening tonight, not from any desire to offend the prejudices of the unenlightened, but in order to make a gesture for British freedom which shall be understood throughout the length and breadth of this glorious empire upon which the sun never sets. Hullo, Tommy. Yes, you'll find a dash of the doings in my office. I hope, Mrs. Greig, that the little ones are quite well. Yes, I am glad to say that the dean has definitely promised to explain how no modern-minded man who respects himself can possibly believe in miracles. Yes, I think, quite a success. Is the colonel keeping well? Fine. Mind, Charlie, no rough stuff on the premises. And if it isn't *dear* Mrs. McLintock. I quite agree. An insult to the memory of those dear ones in whose fast-fading footmarks we unworthily tread. Naughty little twinkle you've got tonight, Ethel. If you can't be good, be careful. As you say, Major, in a one-horse country like Spain… The same to you and many of them."

The brilliant torrent poured itself into the ballroom and split up into little waves of gold and green and scarlet which splashed their way to the small tables set, like snow-capped islands, round the polished floor. There was a great deal of chattering and a great deal of craning to see who was who and in what and with whom was who and a great deal of formal bowings across the gulf which separated ego from ego and immortality from immortality. Of course, there were noisier and less mincing *rencontres,* but these took place for the most part in the newly installed bar on the first floor where three of Mr. J. Shyman Bell's ootchy-looking actressy sort of girls, disregarding Papa Jimmy's instructions about corners, sat on high stools and allowed a very prominent Edinburgh advocate to pay for their drinks. For it was firstly and foremost a social affair; and in Scotland society affairs are always a little grim until drink and music have had sufficient time to make the ladies ignore the ladies.

Amid a burst of applause Mr. J. Shyman Bell, his face falling in rich, crimson folds over his collar and shirt front, appeared on the platform from which the Ohio Octette were to dispense the Katie-I'm-a-kiddin' music favoured by those who find the Psalms of David nonsensical.

"My lords, ladies and gentlemen," his belly rumbled through the other belly that was his face, "I have to thank you from the bottom of my heart for turning out in such numbers tonight. As I look around the hall and see the many distinguished persons who are honouring it with their presence, well, all that I can say is that I am deeply moved. My lords, ladies and gentlemen, I am only a plain businessman. Jimmy Bell, that's my name, Jimmy Shyman Bell without a handle to it; but I think that all my pals would tell you that if there's one man who likes a square deal that man's Jimmy Shyman Bell." He paused to allow for the clapping which he had foreseen. "As I say, my lords, ladies and gentlemen, I'm a plain businessman and, like other plain businessmen, I have to earn my living. And that living, as you all know, I have earned for the past few years by running this Garden of Eden which was, until recently, one of the most popular and the best patronized dance halls in Edinburgh. I'm not what is known as a religious man, but what religion I have is very dear to me and is summed up in the phrase: 'Never do the dirty on a pal.'"

This time the applause was a positive thunder of approval. Stockbroker, chartered accountant, matron, and pretty daughter each in his or her own way felt that they had at least heard the eternal verities intelligibly and pleasantly propounded.

"Now that's a motto that Jimmy Bell's done his best to live up to all his life. Like the next fellow, I've often made mistakes; but I think that I can honestly say that I've never played any underhand trick on one of my fellow men. And it has always been in this spirit of—this spirit of brotherliness and, I may say, affection that I have tried to play my part in the life of Scotland's capital as manager and owner of the Garden of Eden. Judge then of my surprise and consternation when, on the night of the tenth December, this dance hall, which is my sole means of livelihood, was wantonly removed by a Romish priest to this

Bass Rock on which it still stands tonight.

"My lords, ladies and gentlemen, I should be the last person to utter any remarks which might cause offense to our Roman Catholic brethren. Many of us have dear friends who profess that Roman Catholic religion—who profess that Roman Catholic religion which Roman Catholics profess. But I cannot forget that I am a stout Protestant and that my forefathers were stout Protestants and that our dear country Scotland has always made a bold stand for—for stout Protestantism and has ever refused to bend her proud knee before the panoply of Italy's alien yoke." The reverberation of the words pleased Mr. J. Shyman Bell even more than they pleased the audience and he repeated the phrase which he had misquoted from the Pitlochry *Protestant.* "Yes, I say, our dear country Scotland has always refused to bend her proud knee before the panoply of Italy's alien yoke and, if the Pope were to stand before me now in all his jewelled purple and scarlet, I would tell him straight, as man to man, that it is not by stealing away honest men's dance halls that the free-born sons of Caledonia will be induced to be false to the glorious traditions of their history.

"My lords, ladies and gentlemen, at times during the past week I have been tempted to the vain thought that many a man might have chucked up the sponge when he found himself confronted by the fearful odds by which I have been confronted. Imagine the plight of an honest brewer whose brewery was suddenly transferred by gross ignorance and superstition from its accustomed site to the top of the Bass Rock. Or ask yourselves, if you will, what our good-living friends the Edinburgh stockbrokers would have done if their Exchange had been suddenly removed from St. Andrew Square to this same Bass Rock. Ask yourselves these questions, my lords, ladies and gentlemen, and perhaps you will realize the deep despair of your humble servant Mr. J. Shyman Bell when he found himself and his dance hall perched here amidst the foaming billows of the Firth of Forth. But fortunately I have always had a deep devotion to the works of that great poet Rudyard Kipling who has done more to further empire pluck than any other writer alive today. I recalled in my sorrow the glorious lines of his poem 'If' and I resolved to be a man and to go out single-handed and fight the unseen foe. And the result of that resolve is this reopening of the Garden of Eden on its new site as a protest against trickery and treachery the world over.

"My lords, ladies and gentlemen, I appear before you tonight as a suppliant. I want you to tell all your friends about the Garden of Eden on the Bass Rock and of how Jimmy Shyman is making a game fight of it. At the present moment it is impossible to say whether my venture will be a success or a failure. Tonight you are here in your crowds; but unless you continue to come in your crowds I shall be compelled to shut down. I ask you, therefore, to continue to give your old friend Jimmy Bell the support which you have always given him in the past and to believe that here off the coast of North Berwick you will continue to receive the same hearty welcome as you received in Edinburgh."

He had to raise his hand for several minutes before he could continue.

"Tonight, my lords, ladies and gentlemen, is our Grand Opening Night and we are going to be honoured with the presence of the entire chorus of the *Whose Baby Are You?* company who, as you are all aware, were present in this dance hall when it was so craftily removed. At eleven forty-five the Very Reverend the Dean of St. Stephen's, London, is going to broadcast a helpful little talk on miracles and at midnight Miss Gertie de la Muette, the principal girl of the *Whose Baby Are You?* company, will sing her miracle song which is now famous throughout the world and will raffle, in aid of the Rio de Janeiro Bible Society, the silk stockings which she wore during the flight of the Garden of Eden. It is to the generosity of my personal friend Lord Stitcham that we owe the presence of both Miss Gertie de la Muette and her chorus girls. Their performance in Newcastle does not terminate until ten o'clock, but Lord Stitcham, out of the kindness of his heart, has offered to transport them here in his famous fleet of monoplanes.

"My lords, ladies and gentlemen, once again I thank you for your gracious presence and for encouraging me to keep a stiff upper lip and to show those who do not know our ways that Britons never, never shall be slaves. My lords, ladies and gentlemen, once again I thank you and I wish you, one and all, a very pleasant evening's entertainment."

The harvest moon bowed four times, to the immediate front, to the half-right, to the half-left, to the immediate front again and disappeared swiftly on the short, stout body which bore it. Then the music started, gently, like a sensual girl whispering in her sleep, and everybody was in everybody else's arms, dancing, dancing, dancing.

4.

"...AND in these days of general scientific enlightenment no educated man can be expected to believe that matter can transport itself through the ether of its own volition or at the volition of an anthropomorphized hypothesis." The dean's voice came, all wrapped in crackles, out of the invisibility that was London and the more unashamed lowbrows edged on tiptoes towards the bar. "The most elementary acquaintance with the principles of physics will be... ack... iss... ack... oke... vrmp... mediaeval theory of intermittent polytheistic magic is finally untenable... ack... rrtel... prr... nk." Some of the sweeter and younger things looked frankly bored and leaned back felinely and puffed at their cigarettes with a neo-Babylonian expression in their eyes. "To put it bluntly, only an illiterate Spanish or Irish peasant, nurtured in the Roman system of transcendent celestial magic, could accept without reservation the suspension of normal natural laws that is alleged to have taken place fifteen days ago in a country ordinarily famed for the soundness of its porridge and its philosophy...ook...tunk...trek...kwz...suiz..." By this time the bar was filled with stockbrokers and chartered accountants and the sweeter and younger things, more neo-Babylonian than ever about the eyes, were wishing that they could go there too.

By the white sea wall at North Berwick two figures in clothes more black than the night were pacing solemnly.

"The only thing to do, Father, is to ask Almighty God to transfer the whole caboodle to the top of Mount Everest." Canon Geoghegan's voice sounded like rancid pickles being poured into sour milk. "The blasphemy of the whole proceedings astounds me who am accustomed enough to the facile follies of a generation of syncopated adulterers and sons of Belial. To dance wantonly in a place so evidently hallowed by Almighty God! The dog is indeed fond of his vomit. But what beats me is that Plus Bobbie should have yielded without a struggle to that lynx-eyed Italian cardinal, who is incapable through nationality and upbringing of understanding the adjustments of God's economy to local Scottish conditions. If I had been bishop of the diocese I should have bundled the rascal out of my house and have gone to Rome to present in person my case to the Holy Father. But then, as I think I have told you before, you cannot expect much from these consecrated converts. In my opinion, no English-speaking priest is fit to be a bishop unless he is descended from at least three generations of pious Celtic washerwomen."

Father Malachy, who was his companion, tried to stop the sizzling of pickles and milk.

"No, Canon, I do not blame the bishop. As he himself pointed out, it has always been the policy of Rome to matter-of-fact before she miracled, if I may thus express myself. Nor do I blame the cardinal who, after all, was deputed by the Holy Father to examine into the miracle and must therefore presumably have been guided by the Holy Ghost. Indeed I blame nobody but myself who was presumptuous enough to imagine that I could cure by one burst of celestial fireworks what twenty centuries of saintly Catholic lives have failed to remedy. We must obey, Canon; there is no other way out of it. Obedience, as you know, is the supreme rule which the Catholic Church imposes upon all her children. And if we are to place any supernatural interpretation upon the miracle we must interpret it in the light of a rebuke on the part of Almighty God to myself. 'A wicked and adulterous generation seeketh a sign,' Canon, and it is perhaps a wicked and adulterous priest who tries, however pure may be his motives, to upset God's natural laws in order to perform what is ordinarily effected through the Sacraments."

But Canon Geoghegan would have none of it. He protested angrily across the rippling baby waves.

"But, Father, Almighty God Himself permitted you to perform the miracle. You can't get away from that, Father. Why did He allow you to translate the Garden of Eden if it wasn't to further His own supernatural ends?"

"Perhaps He allowed me to do it in order to show me that His ordinary means were best after all." Father Malachy's voice seemed to lull the sea into a shining dark blue pond. "It is certainly a miracle that the Garden of Eden should be on the Bass Rock; but it is equally another miracle that the majority of people should refuse to believe that it is a miracle. No, Canon, Almighty God intended to teach me a lesson and I must say that He's done it pretty thoroughly."

"In that case," said the canon, "faith seems to me to be an unnecessarily hazardous game of supernatural golf in which bunker and hole are liable to become mixed. Upon my word, I can't altogether blame the laity for preferring the cinema to the *Summa Theologica*."

They walked for a few moments without speaking, up and down, up and down on the vague beat which they had still more vaguely chosen.

"I must admit that all this is very hard." Father Malachy waved an indefinite hand in the direction of the cluster of lights on the Bass Rock. "It is not pleasant to see the work of God perverted by the folly of man even when one knows that it is God's Will that it should be so perverted. But I must not again give way to spiritual pride or to the feeling that, if I were Almighty God, I would have ordered things differently. No, Canon, I shall go back to my monastery and be conspicuous only when I sing High Mass in scarlet vestments on the Feast of Saint Blasius of Cappadocia. After all, it is not a Benedictine monk's job to convert modernist clergymen; a monk's job is to sing the Divine Office in choir and so preserve some of the immemorial decencies which the modern world lost when she preferred Hollywood to Rome. And it's a good job, a monk's; for only those are happy who ignore the world and are ignored by it."

Canon Geoghegan waited until Father Malachy's words had gone swinging out to sea like invisible birds which would find no home this side of Australia.

"Father," he said, "I did not bring you down here to discuss generalities which we could have considered more competently and more comfortably in front of the presbytery fire. I brought you down here so that you might see with your own eyes the terrible desecration which was being wrought to your miracle and to persuade you to ask Almighty God to transfer this unhappy dance hall and its revellers to the back of beyond."

Father Malachy laughed softly.

"My dear Canon, I have already told you that I consider that it is God's Will that things should have happened so; and I am afraid that I should be still less popular than I am in Rome if I were to bring off another miracle for everybody to disbelieve in. No, Canon, in the interests of the general welfare of the Catholic Church, I am afraid that I must refrain from meddling."

But the canon, who loathed the Garden of Eden and actresses with a mighty hatred, was not to be dissuaded from persuading.

"Father," he said, "nobody will make me believe that it is in the general interests of the Catholic Church that these unbelieving barbarians should be allowed to make a musical brothel out of a successful miracle. And, as you can't perform the miracle without Almighty God's help, I do not see any harm in asking Him, if it be His holy Will, to transfer all these ruffians and harlots to the back of beyond. All you've got to do, my dear Father, is to pray and to leave the rest to Almighty God."

Father Malachy shook his head.

"No go, Canon," he said ruefully. "I simply daren't suggest anything to Almighty God. The way that He has let this miracle be regarded as a fraud is a sufficient indication of the value which He puts upon my suggestions."

"You needn't make any suggestions," persisted Canon Geoghegan. "All you've got to do is to recite the *Confiteor*, make an act of contrition for what you call your sin of pride, and humbly ask Almighty God, if it be His Will, to transfer the Garden of Eden away from the Bass Rock. You needn't say where; you could leave the choice to Almighty God." The canon edged closer to his companion. "Go on, Father; be a sport. It's our only chance of showing these blasphemers that God is not mocked."

Father Malachy hesitated. After all, it *was* terrible that the Garden of Eden, so honoured by God, should be used as a centre for all the imbecilities of the hour. And there would be that fat Mr. Shyman Bell, with a sleek grin on his red, worldly face, strutting about like a pouter pigeon. And that dreadful song was going to be sung and that famous dean was going to broadcast another wound into the Sacred Heart. Perhaps the canon was right. Perhaps if he were to ask forgiveness God, satisfied that His priest had learned humility, would hear his request.

"The bishop," he began. "He'd be very annoyed if—"

"Damn the bishop," said Canon Geoghegan roundly. "Make your act of contrition like a man and leave the rest to Almighty God."

"And the cardinal. He'd be annoyed, too. And the Pope might deprive me. And my abbot would say that I was getting too much of the limelight and might make me serve in the refectory for the rest of my days. No, Canon, I simply dare not do what you ask me to do."

"Then," said the canon impatiently, "if you're as afraid as all that, just make an act of contrition, ask nothing, and leave everything to

Almighty God."

"But—" began Father Malachy.

"There are no buts," said Canon Geoghegan. "There is only God and that pernicious dancing hall perched like a jade upon the Bass Rock."

Father Malachy yielded.

"All right," he said. "But you must help me to stand the racket if Rome turns nasty."

And with these words Father Malachy took off his hat and handed it to Canon Geoghegan and bowed his grey head in great and silent prayer. He did not know that at that moment Miss Gertie de la Muette was adjusting her short frilly frock in front of her dressing-room mirror and was trying to decide which were the silk stockings she had *not* worn during the flight of the Garden of Eden. He did not know that at that moment the disembodied voice of the dean was croaking: "Roman Catholic clerygmen are rarely English gentlemen and never competent scientists." He did not know that at that moment Mr. J. Shyman Bell, ruddy and round and rollicking, was standing drinks in the bar to the more select retired Indian Army colonels present and was telling them a story which he had heard that morning from a well-known Caledonian hotel lounge lizard. He did not know that the Bee Bee Bee, safely hidden in a corner of the balcony with his Bubbles, was telling her that she was his own wee apple dumpling. He did not know these things because he could not know them and because his mind was shut to God and because he was praying that He would, of His infinite mercy, forgive the pride of a priest who had sought to effect in a day what his Saviour had failed to do in two thousand years. To Jesus, to Mary, to Michael, to John the Baptist, to Peter and Paul he confessed, through them and by them and round them and over them to God; and, as sorrow sped from his heart and crossed the seas and the hierarchies of angels, the Garden of Eden stirred on its foundations, rose slowly and surely into the air, and was absorbed by the night into a cluster of coloured lights which disappeared rapidly in the direction of Edinburgh.

"In conclusion," groaned the voice of the dean as the Garden of Eden came soundlessly and bumplessly to earth opposite the presbytery of the Church of Saint Margaret of Scotland, "if an oecumenical council were to decide tomorrow that the dance hall in question had flown through the air, I should not have the slightest difficulty in believing that it had done nothing of the sort…zk…oke…rrp… tsnk…"

CHAPTER XIII

1.

THE papers made as great a howl over the second miracle as they had over the first. The same theories were advanced and the words "trickery," "mumbo-jumbo," "black magic" were on everybody's lips. Indeed, it was not until the metropolitan dean mounted a special pulpit erected in the middle of the rugby field at Twickenham and loud-speakered to a crowd of eighty thousand that the British public knew exactly what to think. But from that moment all was plain. For, as the dean so clearly pointed out, the fact of the Garden of Eden appearing to have come back to the very place from which it appeared to have disappeared indicated that the Garden of Eden had never been moved at all and that the general public illusion to the contrary had been produced by some hypnotic rote which only served further to establish the Mithraic origins of traditional Christianity. In other words, the so-called miracle might be ascribed to Mithraism masquerading as mediaevalism itself masquerading as modernism. To the majority of the readers of the great dailies the explanation sounded intellectual enough to be true.

So once more the earth went bowling, bowling, bowling. People were as little in Amsterdam as they were in Southsea. Canon

Geoghegan, annoyed that the Garden of Eden had come back to Edinburgh instead of going on to Timbuctoo, returned once more to his hebdomadal denunciations of crêpe-de-chine and Aldous Huxley. Poor Father Malachy went back to his monastery and the life of a choir monk which is, perhaps, so useful because it is so useless. Mr. J. Shyman Bell had to refund a good few thirty shillingses to disgruntled miracle dancers who swore that he had obtained money from them on false pretenses, and Miss Gertie de la Muette and her song were forgotten as quickly as they had been famed. And when, on the Feast of the Epiphany, the naked body (alive) of a famous musical comedy actress was found in the bedroom of a Cambridge professor of applied mathematics, the world heaved a sigh of relief and continued to be, as it has always been, a very muddled sort of place.

THE END

CLUNY MEDIA

Designed by Fiona Cecile Clarke, the CLUNY MEDIA *logo depicts a monk at work in the scriptorium, with a cat sitting at his feet.*

The monk represents our mission to emulate the invaluable contributions of the monks of Cluny in preserving the libraries of the West, our strivings to know and love the truth.

The cat at the monk's feet is Pangur Bán, from the eponymous Irish poem of the 9th century. The anonymous poet compares his scholarly pursuit of truth with the cat's happy hunting of mice. The depiction of Pangur Bán is an homage to the work of the monks of Irish monasteries and a sign of the joy we at Cluny take in our trade.

"Messe ocus Pangur Bán,
cechtar nathar fria saindan:
bíth a menmasam fri seilgg,
mu memna céin im saincheirdd."

Made in United States
North Haven, CT
08 March 2025

66479868R00124